THE GIRL

OF THE

LISTENING HEART

for from Jody
13th Birthday

From THE LIBRARY OF

JANINE MARTIN

©CURRENT, INC.

The Girl
Of the Listening Heart

by

BERTHA B. MOORE

Third Edition

WM. B. EERDMANS PUBLISHING CO.

GRAND RAPIDS, MICHIGAN

1943

THE GIRL OF THE LISTENING HEART
by Bertha B. Moore

—•—

Copyright, 1937, by
Wm. B. Eerdmans Publishing Company

PRINTED IN THE UNITED STATES OF AMERICA
BY J. J. LITTLE & IVES COMPANY, NEW YORK

THE GIRL

OF THE

LISTENING HEART

CHAPTER I

I AM so tremendously thrilled, I just can't keep it all to myself. You see, I have written a story for a contest. When I read that the winning story would bring five hundred whole dollars, I decided then and there to write the winning story.

How I did work! I wrote it in longhand three times, read it out loud to all the family till I knew it almost by heart, and then pecked it out on Dad's old typewriter. Finally, "As Fragrant as Lilacs" was ready to be mailed. Proudly, with my heart thumping a little faster than it ever had thumped, I waited at the mail box for Billy.

When he accepted the precious manuscript, I simply had to say something, I blurted out, "That's a story for a contest. I'm hoping to win five hundred dollars with it!"

He hardly batted an eye. " 'Zat so?" he mumbled, weighing the package. "It'll hafta go first class then."

First class? I wanted to register it, but he didn't think it was necessary to do that. As it was, it cost eighty-nine cents for postage.

He carelessly tucked it into the pocket that carries his out-going mail apparently without realizing how very important it was. Then I stood and watched him carry it off in his old truck. I hardly knew whether to smile or to weep. I could do so much with five hundred dollars!

With a sigh I started back to the house, already feeling grandly victorious, as I tried to imagine just how I would really feel when I carried my check from that very mail box to the house. I don't know why I didn't see him; perhaps the peach tree was in my way, and perhaps I was seeing only a long, slim envelope that contained a long, slim check. Anyway, I bumped spang into Jimmy Casper.

Jimmy is grown up now. We both are. He never lost his lankness, though. He's a whole foot taller than I am and he's straight as a picker-stick and as fat as the proverbial match. No one ever thought of him as being intellectual or literary, but he is right handsome sometimes. He devours farm papers. And his Bible! Why, you'd think there wasn't another book in the world but the Bible, to hear him talk. He never mentions any other reading.

"Hey, Bets!" he greeted me, just as he had always done.

"Hello, Jimmy," I replied, trying to be grownupish. I thought since I was to be a famous authoress and he was no longer a mere boy, because the people at the church had actually elected him to be the Sunday School Superintendent, it was time to begin to show

our ages. And he ought to try to cultivate a little dignity.

"Wasn't that Billy?" he asked, trying to keep up with
me.

"Yes, it was Billy," I replied, seriously. "I sent off my
story."

"So that's what ails you that your little nose is so high
in the air!" he said, tossing his head up and seeing how
high in the air he could make his own nose go.

"You aren't funny," I informed him.

"All joking aside, Bets, I think you are dreadfully
smart to make up a story and write it all out. It's a
real gift.

"Think what a lot of good you could do writing
stories! Bets, you don't know how much I wish you
cared for—well, for spiritual things," he told me softly,
reaching my side and catching hold of my hand.

"As for instance?" I asked, making him release my
hand.

"Take your writing, for instance. Some day you could
be a noted writer of Christian stories. Then think of
what a lot of good you could do," he kept on, sounding
sober and serious.

"I prefer popular fiction," I informed him in my most
magnificent air. "There's more room for my imagination. And really, you know, I like to think of the money
I could make. My ambition is to write till I make some
of the smartest magazines and my novels are known
everywhere, even translated into different languages!"

"Well, you've begun young enough," he said, sighing.

"If you keep at it as most of the other writers have had to do, you may win. But just the same, I wish you would think over what I have just said."

As if he knew about writers and their struggles! I simply could not endure Jimmy another instant; so I excused myself and wandered on to the house. Having completed my task, I felt lost without having "As Fragrant as Lilacs" to work on. It was such a sweet story! Alicia was in love with two perfectly grand young men and three were in love with her. She had a most terrific time deciding which one was to become her companion for life, but she finally chose Richard. They had a perfectly gorgeous wedding with white and pink and purple lilacs banked at the altar in the church, perfuming the entire place. Of course, she was beautiful in her white satin and lace gown and train and veil and huge bouquet of white calla lilies. I still wonder if it would have been better if I had let the bride carry lilies-of-the-valley and freesias and white violets. I had a most trying time, deciding which to use. I looked at the pictures of flowers in seed catalogues galore. Anyway, it was a lovely wedding, just as I dreamed my very own would be some day!

Well, for several days I could not settle down to any serious thinking. I kept expecting something, though I certainly did not know what. Finally a card came, announcing that my story had been received and that it would have a careful reading. If not found available, it would be returned shortly.

Oh, joy! My heart danced, and so did my feet. Jimmy

had been hanging around every evening, and that evening I was nice even to him. I began to lay definite plans for the use of that five hundred dollars!

While I was typing "As Fragrant as Lilacs," I had not realized what a wreck of a machine Dad's old typewriter was. It was simply unusable. I laid some plans. For supper I made Dad's favorite boiled apple pie. I whipped some cream till it could stand alone, and fixed up that pie till it was absolutely irresistible. Did he eat! When he was too full for serious considering and many objections, I popped my plans.

"Will you pay the balance?" was all he said.

"Yes, indeed!" I glibly promised. "I think I'll get a portable so I can take it down by the creek or up in the woods where I can write in perfect solitude."

"Yeah, and the chiggers will eat you up, too," Cherry said, gulping her milk.

I certainly wish someone could teach that child some manners. She is perfectly deplorable! She hears entirely too much and repeats everything that she hears.

That very evening when Jimmy, the inevitable, arrived, my sweet little sister entertained him for me. She did so by informing him that I was going to trade in Dad's old typewriter on a new one that I could carry to Sunday School or the woods or just anywhere and write every time I thought of something to put down. Of course, I suppose Jimmy was very responsive and encouraging so that she would go ahead and tell him all the family secrets. She must have used her imagination, too, for when I consented to tag along with him up to the church where he was to have a meeting with his Sunday School teachers, he asked me all sorts of questions, just as if he were my grandfather or something. It was a perfect evening with a baby moon nestled in the softest of downy clouds. I didn't feel like being talked to in any such way.

"Bets," he asked, "have you prayed about this new career that you are choosing for yourself?"

"Why, certainly, I haven't!" I promptly informed him. "It's a big thing for me, but do you suppose for one minute that I'd bother the Lord about such things when He has the whole world to watch and keep straight?"

"He is as interested in you as He is in anybody or anything. The Bible says that He knows even when one little sparrow falls. It says we are more important than many sparrows. We are taught to pray about our problems. He is not limited in power or in willingness to listen to us. He is like a great, loving, kind father, though He is infinitely more loving, kind, and gentle than any earthly father could possibly be. I wish you believed in prayer. I wish you were a Christian so that you could pray about the new typewriter. It will cost a lot of money."

"What do you think I am? A heathen?" I snapped.

"Not exactly a heathen, but perhaps you had better be a heathen, for then you might have a better excuse for not being a Christian," he said.

"I guess I'm as good as a whole lot of folks that I know."

"You are a whole lot better than many folks that we both know, Bets, but being good hasn't got a thing to do with being a Christian," he had the nerve to tell me.

"Wait till you get to your dear teachers to preach, Mr. Casper. I am tired of being preached to. If I want to write, that's my business. If I want a new typewriter so that I can do better work, that is my business, too. I have made up my mind to write during every spare moment that I have and I need a good machine so that I shan't be losing precious time. This winter I am going to take a course in short-story writing from the university. I am not going at it unprepared, even though I am not praying about it as you seem bent on my doing. The Lord gave me a will of my own, and I intend to use it as I please. Dad's old machine is a piece of junk. I want a shining new one that will be an inspiration to me and that will do perfect writing. I want my work to have a finished, nobby appearance, not cheap and amateurish. Though of course, I needn't expect you to understand!" I concluded, quite grandly, I thought.

Jimmy sighed, and he sounded ancient. "I hope you will not be disappointed in the reception that your work receives. You are young yet. You haven't had time to know much about life. Naturally your stories will sound a little inexperienced, Bets. I just thought it might be a good plan to keep on trying on the old machine until you are surer of yourself. It's not so much fun to be in debt."

And I had been wanting Jimmy to grow up! I

glanced at him in the tender moonlight. He looked like the same Jimmy, really handsome and knightlike, but —his antiquated remarks!

"Thanks for your kind advice, Grandfather. I am sorry that I cannot accept it all. You see, you just don't understand us modern young folks. It was different in your day."

Jimmy actually took hold of my shoulders and shook me! I very nearly bit my tongue!

"Bets, you've just naturally got too much sense to be so utterly foolish and indifferent to the things that really count. Why don't you give up trying to be different from the rest of us and give the Lord Jesus your heart and life? It would be wonderful to all of us and to you yourself just to watch what the Lord Jesus could do with a girl as gifted as you, if she had a listening heart!" he said, sternly.

Well! The more Jimmy Casper talked, the more vexed I became. "Quit your preaching, young man! I'm not ready to give up all the good times that may be ahead of me. I'm not ready to settle down as Ann has done, growing old and sour before my time. Look at your own self. You haven't done a thing but preach to me this whole evening. You didn't used to be like this. You used to be gay and jolly. I haven't heard you laugh like you meant it for ages. Why? You've got religion. That's why! You are the new superintendent of the Sunday School and you must be an example to all the rest of us naughty, wicked little sinners. Good night! I did think you needed to grow up, that you needed to be a little more dignified, but I was mistaken. You sound like old Deacon Tate already. No, sir, I thank you from the depths of my black heart, but I'm not ready to stagnate yet!"

That was a lot of sass. Well, Jimmy had me all muddled. I was determined to have that new typewriter and he wasn't going to be able to say a word that would keep me from having it. No, siree! Hadn't I been forced to make an apple pie for it?

"I am sorry, Betsann. I'll keep still. But I'll not stop praying for you, not as long as I live, until you have surrendered your life to the Lord Jesus," Jimmy said, very softly, and in an altogether different tone.

I actually felt rather meek, but I wouldn't let him know it for worlds.

"Oh, I don't mind your praying for me, but I don't see why you should pester the Lord about a typewriter and my career. When I am older and have seen more of the world than what is around us here in this little bit of back-woods country, I'll settle down and get religion, too. Can't you see, Jimmy, I want to go out and see things and broaden my horizon!"

Jimmy glanced all about him. The baby moon was brighter and a multitude of stars seemed to be protecting it.

"It's pretty broad up here, I think!" he said.

Just then we met Joan and John, two of the teachers in Jimmy's Sunday School, so we didn't argue any more. We were right at the church by that time and he didn't lose a minute getting started. You should have seen and heard him! I was amazed. He went at it as if he had been conducting meetings for Sunday School teachers all his life. At least, it seemed so to me, for he didn't hesitate or lack for ideas or words. It was interesting! If he hadn't been so grandfatherish on the way to the church, I would have told him how much I had admired the way he took hold of things. But I saved it all till some time when he has treated me less like the worst sinner that ever lived in our part of the mountains.

I'm really not so bad. I've always gone to Sunday School, and I've always sung in the choir or played the organ. I have never done anything very dreadful. I don't even pet, for I simply can't stand being pawed over. Mom and Dad would both say that I have been a pretty decent girl. So, why should Jimmy get so worked up just because I don't want to let the corners of my mouth go down and I do want to make the big magazines and be somebody some day? I don't see anything so wicked in that.

The next day I had Dad's old typewriter loaded in Dad's old flivver and then I was ready to start to Charlotte to trade for my swanky new one. As I was about to step on the starter, Jimmy popped up on the running board.

"Where are you going, my pretty maid?" he piped. And he did sound lots more like the old Jimmy than he had the previous night.

"I am not going a-milking, sir," I replied. "Will you

please remove yourself so that I may proceed on my way to Charlotte?"

He actually seemed to wilt. "Bets, are you really going to do it?" he asked.

"Do what?" I asked sweetly, just as if I didn't know exactly what he meant.

"Get the new typewriter?"

"I certainly am going to make the effort."

"I am sorry, but I hope you will not. I came to remind you of John's party tonight. Will you be back?"

I had forgotten all about that old party!

"No, I am staying in Charlotte with Abby tonight," I informed him in my most superior manner.

"But you always lead the games. What shall we do without you?"

"Do? Can't you entertain yourselves without playing kid games? Anyway, if I win that contest, I am not going to stay up here in the woods. You might as well get used to doing without me now," I replied, tossing my head.

"Where will you be, Betsann, if not here?" he asked, meekly, as if he already realized that I was going to be renowned some day.

"Oh, in the city. I shall have to live where I can observe life better than I ever can up here among so few people. I must be going, too. Sorry, Jimmy, to disappoint the crowd, but you can explain to them how important it is for me to be away. Have a good time!" I breezed, stepping on the starter.

"'Bye, Bets! Have a good time, yourself! Be careful how you drive. Remember, you never know what the other fellow is going to do. May the Lord take care of you and bring you back safely!"

"Thanks a lot, Grandfather. And amen!"

I was off. Had I but known what was ahead of me, would I have gone? It's hard to tell. I am so hard-headed that I likely would not have been moved from my determination if I had known that a cyclone would have picked me up and whirled me to the ocean. Maybe it is a good thing we can't see what each tomorrow holds for us. Maybe we wouldn't be brave enough to face some of the things we do face when the time comes.

Well, I didn't know, so I happily gave the old road-ster more gas as we got into the highway, and away I went, singing and as gay as the birds that flitted from tree to tree in the woods all about me. I was dreadfully excited. Yet sometimes I did wish Jimmy hadn't been so solemn and pious. When I stopped to think of some of the things he said, they put a sort of dread in me away deep down. Then I just sang harder and drove faster. Wasn't I on my way to Charlotte, a new type-writer, and fame?

CHAPTER II

IN spite of my dreads and fears I did arrive in Charlotte without even the slightest mishap. I found a store that had typewriters displayed in the windows. And right in front of that store there was a parking space. How fortunate I was! There came to me the thought that maybe back home Jimmy was praying for me and that was the reason that I had gotten along so well and had found the store and a parking space without any trouble at all. But I guess it wasn't.

Of course, I didn't try to carry Dad's old wreck into the store. I made as impressive an entrance as I could. The clerk who came to meet me was positively the best looking young man I had ever beheld. He bowed and he smiled as if he already recognized in me a noted novelist. I explained in my very best manner, I hoped, that I desired a new portable typewriter.

I honestly did not know one machine from another, except that I did suppose those in cases were portables. But he did! He amazed me and confused me, too, with his explanations of differences in values of several different makes. I tried to recall which ones I had seen advertised the most and finally settled on a very shining, perfectly beautiful, restful green machine that shut up like an overnight bag. In fact, my handsome clerk assured me that the case with the machine removed, could be used as such a bag. Imagine a bargain like that!

"Cash?" my Sir Knight asked, smiling as he held his pencil poised in the air.

Cash! Inwardly I gasped. Trying to be brave and equal his smile, I explained about Dad's old junk heap out in the car, though I certainly was ashamed to have him see it or the old dowdy car either. Well, he went out and brought in the remains of a perfectly good typewriter. He allowed me fifteen dollars on it!

"Is the balance cash?" he asked, smiling again, as he awaited my reply.

"Do you ever give time on the balance?" I managed to ask.

"Oh, yes," he replied. "Whenever we are sure the customer is reliable. Can you give references?"

References? Again I gasped, inside. Dad? Jimmy? Our preacher? Whom could I give?

"Do you reside in the city?" he asked, before I could decide upon my reference.

"No, I live—out of town!" I replied. I had almost said, "On a farm away back in the hills!" "But I have a cousin who lives in this city."

"What does he do?" he wanted to know.

What did Joe do? He sold something. I remembered that, for Abby had spoken of his selling. Well, a merchant is one who sells. Therefore, Joe must be a merchant.

"He is a merchant," I ventured.

I gave Joe's name and address. The clerk seemed highly satisfied and there was a funny twinkle in his charming grey eyes, I recalled at a later time.

"And now about the payments, Miss ——," he hesitated.

"Miss Elizabeth Ann Ellison," I enlightened him.

"Ah, yes, as I was saying, Miss Ellison, will ten dollars a month be all right for your payments?"

How could a girl on a farm ever earn ten dollars a month? I felt suddenly very weak, for I could just see myself returning home with Dad's old typewriter beside me. And then how Jimmy would talk! Then I remembered "As Fragrant as Lilacs"!

"That's all right," I replied, tremendously relieved. "You see, I am really expecting to pay the entire amount very soon. My publishers are considering a story now."

You should have seen his eyes! We finally got everything all settled and I was being followed to the door by my perfectly gorgeous new typewriter. There, bowing and smiling, the clerk handed me the machine and said, "It has been a pleasure to serve you, Miss Ellison. Do call again!"

I can't begin to express my feelings as I somehow got into that shabby roadster. I believed I was actually beginning to live my new life. I decided right then and there to have a new car with some of my very first earnings.

I could have driven home, but it's such fun to stay with Abby and Joe. And then, I really wanted Jimmy and the bunch to see what would happen if I were not at their silly party. I went to Abby's.

We had a marvelous evening. Joe drove us all around Charlotte. We went to a movie. I don't know whether I exactly liked it or not. Some of it I did and some I didn't. I don't see why women have to drink and smoke in a picture in order to be entertaining. It's anything but entertaining to me. But, on the other hand, it really added another spark to my ambition. Just as soon as I became well enough known, I'd write a really worth-being-seen screen story. After we had devoured ice cream and candy and popcorn, we finally went home. I was too full of ideas and thoughts to sleep, but finally I did. I dreamed that Jimmy was waiting for me, worried because of what I might have done while I was in Charlotte. The idea!

The next day the weather was perfect and I thoroughly enjoyed the homeward trip, though I really did not see a thing but the road ahead of me. I was planning a screen story. I would make oodles of money if I could write for pictures! Then I imagined various ways that I would show Mom and Dad and even Cherry my, *my* very own new typewriter. Oh, of course, since Dad's old wreck was traded in on it, I'd let him have a share in the new one and use it whenever he wanted to—if I were not too busy with it.

Quite safely I arrived home, as hungry as a bear. Almost as soon as I had arrived, Jimmy poked his head into our sacred family circle as I was demonstrating my new machine to the family.

"It certainly is a beauty, Bets. How much does a doings like that set a person back?" he asked, inelegantly.

That clerk had used such perfect English!

"It cost fifty dollars," I replied, icily, not telling him a word about the trade or the balance due.

He whistled. "Half as much as a mule is worth!"

I felt cold chills of repulsion go up and down my spinal cord. But then I really did not expect anything else from Jimmy. He has always been in these mountains and his horizon certainly is not very broad.

The next day I tried to compose myself and concentrate upon my career as a writer, but all the time I'd think about that clerk, that drive around Charlotte, the movie! While I was wishing I'd have to go back soon, and not succeeding in jotting down a single word, Mom called me to go to Aunt Millie's after a pattern for a dress for Cherry. Back to earth I flopped. Back to earth I stayed for one whole, entire month. It was hoeing time, and never did I see such weeds. Every day I expected to hear from my "Lilacs," but no word came. It must take forever for judges to reach their final decisions in contests. Then I remembered the card said the manuscript would be returned soon if not found available.

"Fragrant as Lilacs" must have won!

I really did not mind hoeing while I waited for my check. Jimmy kept hanging around. He always wanted to know if I had heard from my story. I wondered sometimes if he wanted to borrow some money!

Then along toward the end of the month, Billy brought THE LETTER. I had absolutely forgotten. It was past time for the second payment on my typewriter. The company would appreciate an immediate payment.

I had exactly thirty-seven cents. Why didn't the publishers send my check? I didn't dare ask Dad for a cent, for he had not been any too well pleased with that "balance due." Jimmy always managed to have a little cash, but I certainly did not want him to know I was so deeply in debt when he had been so free with his warning advice. I was simply desperate. Finally I wrote the company that I would call at my earliest convenience.

That was the first time in my life, I think, that I wished I could pray, that I wished I really knew if God were interested in our problems as Jimmy had assured me He was. I wished I knew more about Jimmy's God. I guess I wished He were my God, too.

"What are you writing these days, Betsann?" asked Jimmy the very night after I had sent off the letter to the company.

"I haven't had time to write anything. Don't you

know how hard I have had to hoe? When I do get a minute I am too dead tired to think. One can't write unless she is in just the right mood, and one can't get in that mood if she has to hoe till her back is broken and her hands are blistered," I informed him, tragically.

He looked at my hands. They were not blistered, but they were not as soft as they had been in the early spring.

"Poor Betsann!" he said, so pitifully that he made me furious. Then he asked, "Did you ever try writing a juvenile?"

A juvenile?

"Just what do you mean?" I asked, jerking my hand away.

"A story for children. In lots of farm papers there is a page for children and their stories are always right interesting. Now you have a way with you when you tell stories to Cherry and her bunch. Why don't you try writing some of the stories that you tell them?"

I began to forgive him. "I have never thought about that," I had to acknowledge.

"I'll bring over some samples and let you see what they are like. If you were a little more interested in Sunday School work, I'd suggest stories for Sunday School papers. They would give you good practice in writing and expressing your thoughts on paper."

"Why, Jimmy, I'd have to have a Bible at my elbow and some one to tell me where to find the verses to use and explain to me what they meant. I want to write about life and living!" I informed him.

"You evidently do not read many Sunday School papers. There is nothing dead or dull about them. Talk about life and living! One doesn't know life; one doesn't begin to live until he begins to read and to study his Bible. I'll tell you, Bets, since I've had my job as superintendent, I've done more reading and more studying than I ever did before in all my life put together. I'm just beginning to find out what I have been missing. If you don't study your Bible, you are missing a lot, too. Why, Bets, it's the greatest example of literature in the world! You should study it from a literary viewpoint for your own enlightenment as a writer. It has the loveliest poetry in it that you have ever read. And there's a perfect love story in the Book of Ruth. I hate to have you miss so much, Betsann!" Jimmy finally added.

It was the first time I had ever heard Jimmy wax so eloquent and I was really moved. I was not ready to acknowledge it, though. I did not want him to win his victory too easily. "I'm glad you like it, Jimmy, but what I need to do is to study the leading current magazines and novels if ever I am going to write for them. I haven't time for Bible reading, too."

"What do you know about 'night caps' and 'cocktail parties' and girls who smoke cigarettes and drink along with the boys and a lot of rotten stuff that your leading magazines tell in their stories that are written by your noted authors? Last week I read one through that did not have a single story without something in it about drinking, petting, girls smoking, or dancing through doors to terraces, leaving it to the reader's imagination as to what happened next. Could you have written a story for that magazine?" Jimmy asked, dreadfully in earnest.

"I could learn if I had half a chance to see life away from here," I told him.

"May the dear Lord keep you from having the slightest chance!" he replied. "Why, Betsann, it simply isn't in you. You can't write what is not you. You are too pure, too fine, too honest even to think of trying to learn how to write such stuff."

"Jimmy, I'm not absolutely dumb. I could learn a lot about life without having to live like those folks live. Don't you suppose I could use my eyes and ears? I learned some things while I was with Abby this last time."

"Why don't you make a study of life up here in these mountains? There are examples of all sorts up here. You know that as well as I do. Here we don't call a drink from a bottle of bootleg whiskey a cocktail and when a bunch of men and women get drunk, we don't say they were at a cocktail party. We think of them as beneath us, as needing our prayers and our help, as fit subjects for the law to deal with. But for my part, I can't see that they are one bit different from the moneyed society imbibers that you and others make heroes of. Betsann, they are not your kind. Just as these up here are not your kind. I have heard you object just as hard as the rest of us to the bootlegging and blockading that is going on. You have seen the results of liquor in these hills as plainly as I have in the broken homes, the drunken young men and boys who come to church and make the whole house smell like an old swill barrel. You were as hurt and disgusted as any one when you heard that little nine-year-old Sue got drunk last Sunday afternoon. Don't you see?"

I saw! But I wasn't ready yet to let him know how much I was seeing. "Oh, Jimmy, don't fuss so! You've never been any place but up here in these woods till you are as narrow as most of these valleys are. Since you have become so serious and pious, you aren't a bit of fun. You talk like an old fogy. But please don't try to make one out of me. Bring on your precious farm papers with their stories for children. But let me do as I please with my career," I told him, and I certainly meant that much.

He was beginning to make me feel as if I were about to commit a crime if I even tried to write a story for a real magazine. I am sure I have read stories in some magazines that have been quite uplifting and have really made me want to do better.

Finally he departed and I was alone with the problem of a payment on my typewriter to solve. I decided to try a story for children. I read and read farm papers until I had devoured every one he had brought. Then I wrote my three favorite stories, the three that Cherry and her bunch liked best. I sent them off rather fearfully. Then I began to wait again. I kept on waiting. I did not hear from "Fragrant as Lilacs." I did not hear from any of the three stories. At the end of a month two of the stories had found their way back home. I was desperate. I lost my appetite. Jimmy kept me provoked because he could see that something was wrong and he kept wanting to know what it was.

Then came the second letter. Another payment was due! If I did not make a substantial payment at once the company would have to take legal action, or call upon my reference! Legal action! Would they have me arrested? What would Joe do? I had neglected telling him I had used his name. By mail time the following day I was ready to confess all to Jimmy and borrow five dollars to make a payment that would perhaps keep them from legal action. But glory be! There was a check for $15.75 for the third story. I felt like shouting as some of the old women do in the annual revival we have at our church.

"There! I just knew you ought to write for children and not this high-brow grown-up stuff!" exclaimed Jimmy, when I showed him the check. "You don't know it, of course, but I have been praying a lot about your writing. I do praise the Lord for this answer to my prayers!"

I don't think the Lord had anything to do with the story. It was one that I have told and told to the children. I told Jimmy so, too. He seemed actually hurt because I didn't give the Lord any credit for it.

"Your father and I think you might as well stay a week in Charlotte with Abby. You have been working pretty hard, and a change will do you good," Mom said, after I had told them that I was going to pay fifteen dollars on the typewriter.

A week with Abby! How perfectly thrilling! I'd see life! I'd really live that week.

"If you were not going to stay so foreverish, I'd go along and buy myself a new suit of clothes," Jimmy told me the evening before I was to start to Charlotte. "Sis knows a girl in Asheville who is coming to visit her. Naturally, Sis wants me to dress up, but I say overalls are good enough for any girl. Sis just sasses when I say so, for she says this girl is some class and that she is used to seeing young men dressed like gentlemen. She must be like a girl in some of those stories you want to write. You really had better come back sooner than you expect and make a study of her, Betsann."

"She is right!" I told him, ignoring all that he had said about the Asheville girl. "Some girls like to see a man in something besides overalls. When is she coming?"

"Friday. Don't ask me when she is leaving."

"Who cares?"

"I do!" he declared. "It'll be a nuisance having a strange girl under my heels all the time."

"I thought she was coming to visit Marjorie," I said, yawning.

"I can't remain unseen all the time. Betsann, you'll drive carefully and be a good girl while you are gone. Won't you?" he asked, picking up his old cap, having observed, I supposed, my yawning.

"Yes, sir, Grandfather. I'll not make the old car go over fifty and I promise to be in bed every morning by three. Be your age, Jimmy!" I advised.

"Well, I want you to have a good time, but I want it to be the right kind of a time. And well, you may not be the least bit interested in knowing it, but I'll be praying for you every day that you are away," Jimmy said, so solemnly that you would have thought he was a preacher.

"That's sweet and thoughtful of you, Jimmy, but I suspect you'll be so busy keeping your company from under your heels that you will forget all about me. I hope you will have a good time, too, and—well, the right kind of a time, you know!" I replied, just as sweetly as I could and I smiled.

Jimmy did something that he had never done in all his life before. I'm sure I didn't like it, too, and I felt like slapping him good and plenty, but he was gone before I had fully recovered.

"Take that, you tease!" he said, as he jerked me to him and kissed me. Just once! He didn't have the chance to do it the second time.

Well, he was gone. I really did wonder what the Asheville girl would be like. Marjorie is pretty grand herself, though she is rather pious, too.

The next morning I packed carefully, although that didn't mean much to me, for country girls seldom have many clothes that will do for city wear, especially when visiting a cousin as gay as Abby is. I hummed happily as I dressed, for I was full of eager anticipations. I was going to see real life for a whole week!

When I was ready to start, I even kissed Dad, and he seemed pleased. Then I was off, off to a big city, off to a new life, off to study people so that I could really write for the sort of magazine I wanted to make.

I would have been frightened stiff if I had known what was ahead of me in that week. And what was ahead of Jimmy! Several times as I drove blithely along, I wondered what the girl would be like and how hard Jimmy would fall. But I determined not to let anything spoil my week. Not even the fact that Jimmy had said that he would pray for me every day!

CHAPTER III

HOW can I ever write all about that week in the city of Charlotte? It seemed shorter than a week, yet it seemed much longer, for so many, many things happened.

I drove directly to Abby's. I parked the old family roadster in their extra garage, and didn't take it out again until I started home. Abby drove their new coupe that was as shining as my new typewriter, and I felt grand and important as I sat there beside her. I did wish Jimmy and Marjorie's company and just everybody back home could see me. We had to park in a parking lot and walk to the store where I had bought the typewriter.

I wondered if the same clerk would wait on me and if he would recognize me. I did hope I could make an extra good impression on Abby. Sure enough, he came towards us as we entered!

"Why, hello, Rust!" Abby exclaimed. "I didn't realize this is where you earn your daily bread."

I gasped. Abby knew him!

"Hello, yourself, Abby!" he replied, smiling upon

Abby with his glorious smile and absolutely ignoring my presence. "What crying need brings you here?"

"I came with my cousin. Let me present her to you. Miss Ellison, Rust. She bought a typewriter here once upon a time."

I was so surprised that I blurted out, "Oh, we have met before. He sold me my typewriter." Then I could have bit my tongue.

"Oh, sure! Why, yes, Miss Ellison, we've met before," stammered Abby's Rust. "What can I do for you today, Miss Ellison?"

I overcame my chagrin and announced that I had brought in fifteen dollars to pay on my debt. He was delighted. He surely would not have been much more courteous if I had paid every penny I owed.

And Abby invited him to her house! He accepted her invitation most heartily. He asked if he might bring Bob along and another girl. Abby said for him to do that by all means.

I was all a-flutter as we drove home. Abbey explained that they had not known Rust very long, but that he seemed to be a smart young fellow, and that he was buying a junior partner's share in the business. Some day he would be a first class business man. She did not know the Bob that was to come with him and had no idea who the girl would be.

What should I wear?

"Never mind. We'll find something for you to wear," Abby assured me.

And she did! Abby has the loveliest clothes and is

about my size. Since everything was new to me, I was perfectly thrilled with every frock she suggested. That first night I wore a yellow frilly stiff creation that made me feel like a butterfly. I even wore her slippers, little black pumps.

"You certainly look precious," she said, as she whirled me around. "No one would ever think you came from the hills."

If only Jimmy could have seen me!

But it was Rust who saw me first. I did my best not to be self-conscious, but I had a hard time acting as if I were used to it.

The girl—they called her Kitten—was a wee slip of a girl with the blackest, slickest hair I ever saw. It was cut in a straight bob and she wore it severely back, tucked over one ear and the other one covered with a sprig of it. I mean her black hair! On the exposed ear she wore a huge, red, glistening ear-bob. Around her slender throat were red, glistening beads. Her frock was white and her slippers were white. Her lips were as red as her beads and so were her finger tips. They made me shudder. Abby had put some "make up" on me. She wouldn't let me have much red in my cheeks and just a touch of red on my lips.

"Betsann," she had said, "I never could stand to see a girl with so much on her skin that no one could tell whether her face had been washed or merely smeared with face creams. You will be much more attractive, I am sure, if you aren't made up to look like the old-fashioned comic valentines that we used to slip in the desks of the kids we didn't like at school. No boy wants a painted doll. He wants a real live girl that won't rub off if he does happen to touch her. I know Joe fusses if my powder rubs off on his coat sleeve!" She said she detested bloody looking finger nails, and so she used a polish that merely tinted my nails.

"So you won't look anaemic," she said.

Kitten certainly didn't look anaemic. She looked feverish!

Bob was to have a career, too. He was a poet. He was even handsomer than Rust, with enormous, soulful brown eyes. He reminded me of old Shep when he looks up at me, begging for something. Bob didn't always have his eyes wide open. In fact, he kept them rather dreamily closed as if he were listening to the Muse inspiring him to higher and higher flights of poetic fancy.

"Do you play bridge?" asked Bob.

"No, I don't play bridge," I had to acknowledge. My, I was dumb! At first I could think only of real bridges. Then I came to my senses and remembered seeing pictures of bridge parties in the magazines and of reading about the game.

"I'm glad you don't!" Bob said, soberly. "It's a stupid game. I much prefer just watching the expressions on the faces of those who play."

"Oh, do you study people, too?" I asked.

"When I find someone who is interesting enough. Most of them bore me to death."

I wondered if I were a bore. He did not seem to think so.

While we sat around and became acquainted, Abby and Rust and Bob planned the whole week. One night, a dinner to be followed by a movie; another night, a ride away out in the country to some funny place for dinner and dancing; another dinner at Rust's club to be followed by another movie; a concert of some kind, and finally a dinner and dance at Abby's. Oh, it all sounded perfectly thrilling to me! But I was inwardly a little frightened. I shall have to confess to that in order to be honest, and I have always prided myself on being absolutely honest. I actually wondered what Jimmy would say if he knew the plans. I wondered if he would pray a little harder if he knew about the dances and movies. But outwardly I was as jubilant as Cherry is at Christmas.

Joe shoved the furniture against the wall and kicked the little rugs into corners and we danced. That is, they danced. I am sure I don't know what to call what I did. I didn't suppose I was dancing, for I did not know one step from another; but Rust and Bob both assured me that I was learning more quickly than any girl they had tried to teach! If I were, there was not much to learn, for all I did was let myself be pulled around and swept from side to side by the one who happened to be smothering me. I was not at all sure that I liked dancing. When I told Abby so after they had gone, she just laughed.

"You'll get used to it. It is all rather new to you now.

You will be telling me a different story by the time your week is up," she said.

"Maybe!" I replied, not at all sure.

Abby told me that we were to dine and dance—that sounded like the greatest adventure that I could ever have! Dine and Dance!—at one of the most fashionable places in the whole city that next night. I had confided in her about my ambition to write and to write for the very best magazines that were published. She had agreed that I should observe the sort of life that I wanted my characters to live. She dressed me up in a perfectly gorgeous, perfectly backless, perfectly slippery, white crepe evening gown. Oh, did I feel undressed! How I had admired those very same gowns in the fashion pages of the magazines that were my special favorites. I'd even preened before my mirror in my nightgown, imagining I was a girl who was going to a great reception. But the real thing! My spine felt all creepy. If Jimmy could have seen me, I do believe he would have taken off his coat and simply forced me to put it on. Abby made all sorts of fun of me. She said no one would notice how undressed I was, for they would all be just like me, but if I were well covered, then I would attract attention. She was as barebacked as I was. And of course, sleeveless. Well, I was thankful that it was a warm night and that no one from home was there to see me.

It was as Abby had said. The girls and even the old women were all in extremely long skirts! No one seemed to look twice at me, except Bob and Rust. Rust told me I certainly did look keen. Bob said I was divine. I felt better.

We ate and drank. I mean, a lot of folks certainly drank, and ate some. So much silver and so many dishes were confusing. And such crowds! I wasn't hungry, but I *was* thirsty. There was a tall, perfectly beautiful glass by my place that I supposed was water, for the stuff in it was clear and white. I started to take a good drink of it and nearly choked to death. It wasn't water! I didn't risk another sip of anything. I did not take many bites of food either, but watched the people.

All over the great room were girls not a bit older than I am and some not as old, who were smoking and drinking. It made me rather sick to watch them. Yet I knew I had to get used to this sort of thing if it were to be my life. I told myself over and over that it was because I was so green and ignorant that it was repulsive to me.

It seemed as if we sat at the tables for hours. Between courses some of the folks danced and there were some special entertainers who sang and danced on a raised platform that was near our table. The songs were all about love and were sung in the most lovesick voices imaginable. They certainly were different from our mountain ballads that tell about the fights someone has for his beloved and all sorts of valiant things a fellow would do for the girl he loved. And we sing them in good old rousing choruses, not in a whine that makes a person's spine creep, like a hound dog howling in the middle of the night. I can't say that I was very crazy about the special attractions. But I wasn't educated up to them! I hoped that I would learn to like them, for they must be the very latest and best things.

Well, by the time that dinner was over, Rust was too gay for words. He could hardly stand up and he insisted that I dance with him. I was so mad I could have popped, but I was also perfectly helpless. Abby had drunk every drop of that terrific chokey stuff and was acting downright mean. Joe was acting cute, trying to flirt with every girl near him. Bob was as cool as a cucumber on ice. He sat with a perfect scowl on his face as he watched the people. I wondered if he were making up a poem about Life. I almost slapped Rust while we were dancing because he was holding me so tight I was uncomfortable. When I told him so he merely grinned and squeezed tighter. Then I told him if he were not gentleman enough to know how to treat a decent girl, I'd certainly never go anywhere with him again and what was more I'd go back home the very next day. He mumbled something under his awful breath and let me loose.

It certainly seemed to me that going-home time never would come. I was miserably tired and sleepy. You see, I was sober and there must not have been many others who could have said the same thing truthfully. But finally Abby found me and asked if I were ready to go home. Rust was to have taken me, but Abby told him quite frankly that he was too drunk to

be trusted and that she and Joe would take me home.
Was I thankful!

And this was Life!

Poor Joe! He had to go to work the next morning,
but Abby and I stayed in bed. Oh, by the way, Joe is
a traveling man. He does sell something, but he isn't
a merchant. I haven't yet told him that I used his name
for a reference.

Joe was to be away from home the rest of the week.
Well, I slept till about one and after a bath and a big
breakfast-dinner, I felt keen. But Abby still looked like
a wreck and said her head ached. No wonder! If I had
drunk that glass of fire-water, I'd have been dead to the
world for a week!

That night was the night for dinner at Rust's club
with a movie after it. Abby was to go and Bob was to
bring an extra man for her as well as a girl for himself.
I couldn't help wishing that I was to be Bob's girl instead of Rust's because Bob hadn't been so drunk the
night before.

I tried to think of Jimmy as one of the crowd at that
dinner-dance, but I just couldn't get him fixed into the
picture. He would have been a lot better looking than
most of the fellows had been, but he simply wouldn't
fit. That's how narrow he is! Would I ever again fit in
the pokey play-parties back in the hills?

Abby did her best with me for that night. I wore a
very vivid green that was subdued a little with black
velvet bows and a sash. It didn't have any back either,

but Abby said that I had a perfectly beautiful back. Maybe I have, but I like it covered a little.

Rust didn't seem to remember that he had been drunk the night before. He didn't say a word about it. Acted as if he had never tasted a drop in his life. He brought me a cute round bunch of tiny pink rosebuds to wear on my shoulder. There was so little that covered my shoulder that I was almost afraid we'd have to glue the flowers on, but Abby managed to pin them to the little narrow strap of black velvet that was there. Rust said I was beautiful, and he told me over and over again that he had never guessed when I bought my typewriter from him that so soon I should mean such a lot in his life. He kept telling me how the whole world would appreciate me and my wonderful talent some of these days. Of course, I rather liked to have him say a lot of the things he said, even though I did rather suspect that he didn't mean them all.

The man Bob brought for Abby was rather middle aged, handsomer than either Bob or Rust, a regular man-of-the-world. He wore the most perfectly fitting clothes that I had ever seen on a man and his manners were simply magnificent. He treated Abby as if she were a queen and me as if I were a real princess. I wished right away that I was to be his companion for the night, for I just knew he must be dreadfully intellectual and that he must know all about Life. But he was Abby's and I was to be in the crowd with them.

Bob's girl was different from Kitty, too. This one was older, more experienced, more daring. She was tall, thin (back home we'd have said she was plumb skinny), and very stately. I learned that she, too, was a writer, but that she was a public stenographer, also, which gave her a wonderful opportunity to study people. She had her own little apartment where she could invite just the friends she wished to have at whatever hour she wanted them. I liked her a lot—at first. I wasn't so sure by the time I was back home.

Rust must be a rising young business man, for his club was very elegant, I thought. We had a special table. The food was really good and I was as hungry as I am at home after a day of hoeing in the cotton patches. This time I didn't mistake the wine for water because it was red wine. They all insisted that I drink mine, but I was determined that I was going to stay myself, so that I could study these people about whom I wanted to write. Why, these were the folks that the leading magazine stories were about! I tried to decline as graciously as I could, and I stuck to it. Anyway, I never did like the smell of liquor, much less the taste of the stuff, and I certainly don't like the effects. I've seen too much of it back in the hills. But the rest of our crowd drank; Bob did, his girl did, Abby did, and even Norman did. And Rust! He emptied his glass first.

Between courses they smoked. I was about to accept a cigarette and take a wee puff or two when I noticed how yellow Bob's girl's fingers were. I wondered how much one would have to smoke to become as stained as she was. I refused, telling them that I never smoked when I was eating because I didn't like the flavor tobacco gave to food.

"Don't insist, Bob. She is a rare jewel. It isn't often one meets a girl who enjoys food more than a good cigarette. It's refreshing to my jaded soul," said Patricia, coming to my rescue.

I was grateful until I happened to catch the expression in her eyes. Then I simply hated her. I'd have smoked a dozen cigarettes right then and there if I hadn't been too scared that I'd be sick and have to go home. Her jaded soul! I doubted if she had a soul. If she did, I didn't doubt but that it was jaded all right.

Then I remembered that I was studying Life and drew in my horns and proceeded to be as gracious as I could be. But again I was glad when dinner had ended. I was glad that I was a stranger in that city, for we were a noisy crowd who left the place and went to a movie. I wondered what would happen there, if they should disturb the house, but it is strange how sometimes even drunk folks can behave when they know they should.

I don't suppose Jimmy would have called it behaving. Norman openly held Abby's hand and she leaned her head on his shoulder and dozed a good deal of the time. Rust tried putting his head on my shoulder, but I didn't like the touch of his moist hair on my bare shoulder and I didn't like the whiff of his breath. I made him sit up like a gentleman. The least said about Bob and Pat, the soonest mended. The picture was pretty good, but it showed just what I had been seeing.

I wasn't in any mood to enjoy more of Life, so I sat there and wondered what Jimmy and Marjorie's company were doing!

It was nearing the break of day when we finally got to bed. I was so fagged that I wondered if I should be able to go to Pat's apartment for dinner that night and a concert afterwards. A concert! I was thankful that it wasn't a dance or a movie as I finally drifted off to sleep.

The minute I opened my eyes I beheld the letter that the maid had placed on the table beside my bed. It was from home, but it wasn't Mom's writing. It wasn't Dad's. It wasn't Cherry's. It was Jimmy's! There was the queerest feeling in my heart as I realized it was Jimmy's letter. Was he going to announce his engagement to Marjorie's company? My fingers fairly trembled as I tore open the envelope. Then I read it:

"Dear Betsann:

"We are missing you. Are you going to stay the whole week? Libby Lou is the grandest girl you ever saw. Hurry home so you can become well acquainted with her.

"Don't forget that I said I would pray for you every single day while you are away. I haven't forgotten. I am praying for you and for some reason I can't help but feel that you are needing prayers. God keep you from yielding to the many temptations that may come to you there.

"Hadn't you better come on home?

"Marjorie sends love. She said she wished you were here to help her entertain Libby Lou, though she doesn't seem to need much entertaining.

"So hurry home.

"To

"JIMMY."

I did the silliest thing. I cried and cried till my nose was a sight and my eyes were all red. I was so homesick I could have died right then and there. Then I came to myself and realized that Libby Lou was there with Jimmy and it was up to me to do all I could during the rest of the week to prepare myself for the career that was before me.

I proceeded with the preparation!

CHAPTER IV

CAN'T we have the biggest ambitions and then have them smashed quick? As I dressed to go to Pat's apartment, I thought how perfect her life must be, for she lived absolutely alone, she did exactly as she pleased, in short, she was perfectly independent. And she was still very young, Abby thought, around twenty-two or three.

I wore yellow that night. It was not such a backless dress, and I was a lot more comfortable in it, though I did wish I had more room when I moved around. It fitted me so quick that I was afraid I'd burst the seams, but Abby laughed and said I had no idea how elastic the material was. It was a good thing!

I can hardly describe Pat's apartment, for it was the very first one I ever saw. To me it was perfectly gorgeous. There was a dear living room done in red and white! It was startling at first, but as I became accustomed to it I realized that it must be very, very elegant. Her bedroom was in orchid with maple furniture. A perfect dream of a room. All about the place was an illusive, subtle fragrance. I discovered incense burning in the most cunning little containers. At first I was positively thrilled, and began to plan my own apartment that I, too, should have some day.

Then the fun began! There were cigarettes on every table in every room. Abby smoked more than I had known she did. I had forgotten to try a cigarette before I left home, so I didn't dare spoil the night by trying one there. Again I declined the drinks that were served before we ate.

"You go to Sunday School, don't you, Elizabeth Ann?" asked Pat.

My face burned. I wanted to shout no, that we did not have Sunday Schools where I lived! Her tones had been sugar-coated as she asked the question. I am sure I turned as red as an early beet.

"Why, yes, everybody goes to Sunday School at home. It is a place for us to go," I replied, and then felt as mean as Peter must have felt that first time he had denied the Lord. Why hadn't I held up my head and said, "Yes, indeed, I go to Sunday School every Sunday and preaching whenever we have it?"

"I didn't think your innocence was put-on," cooed Pat, smiling at me as if I were an infant.

Rust came to the rescue.

"Lay off Betsann, Pat. She writes stories and books and some day she will be making you a villain in a story," he said.

"Silly, the villain is always a man," Pat told him, scornfully, ignoring entirely the fact that I was to have a career.

"Then she will make you the viper," he persisted.

Pat smiled and put her long arms about my shoulders, "She will make me a harmless, pure virgin. Won't you, darling?" she cooed.

I wanted to shake her off and push her against her own white wall, but I realized in time that I was studying Life and smiled back as she smiled at me. "I'll make you an angel," I replied, sweetly.

Dinner was announced by the waitress, hired for the occasion. It was served in the living room because there wasn't room for six of us in the wee breakfast nook. I decided that my apartment should have a dining room that would accommodate at least eight! But I doubted if I'd have cigarettes all over and I knew I'd not have liquors anywhere.

Well, I had thought the other dinners were gay, but they were tame compared to this one. They all seemed to drink more than they ate. I was busy keeping Rust's hands off me. I hate being handled by sober men, but I loathe the touch of a man who has been drinking. Bob told Rust to behave or he'd throw him out and that made Pat mad. Abby was too busy with Norman to know I existed. What would Joe have said, I wondered.

Suddenly I remembered that Jimmy was praying for me! With the realization of that fact, I became more calm, less worried. I was able to endure what took place. And finally all the liquor that Pat had must have been drunk, for no more was served. I was thankful for that. After her soft white rugs had been dumped in a heap for dancing and the radio had blared forth more dance music than the other tenants in the building could have wanted, someone remembered the concert. I was really the only one who seemed to want to go, but the boys had bought the tickets and we went. Thus ended that night. The fresh air revived them somewhat and we were a more respectable bunch than we had yet appeared.

And then it was finally the last night before I was to take Dad's old car back home so he could go to our little town on Monday. It was the night of Abby's dinner dance.

"Abby, please don't have anything to drink. I mean any liquor," I begged. "I am sick and tired of seeing this crowd get tipsy every night."

Abby laughed. "Have you seen enough of that side of life?" she asked.

"Yes, I have! I'd like to see what a sober crowd would be like," I replied, jumping at that as an excuse.

"All right. Since it is to be your party, I'll let you have your way, but the bunch may think it's a dull time they are having. And don't blame me if they carry their own stuff with them. They do a lot of times."

"That won't be your fault. I'll not blame you a bit," I promised, tremendously relieved.

If I had been dressed up before, or rather undressed up, I was more so for that last occasion.

"I want you to look your very, very best," Abby said, as she laid out the most delicate creation in orchid chiffon that ever I had beheld, even in display windows. "There will be a new couple here tonight. The man is a rising young lawyer and the girl one of our high school teachers."

I can't begin to tell you how thrilled I was. For one evening at least I was to mingle with people who were really intellectual, a lawyer and a high school teacher! Of course, Rust was intellectual, for he was a rising young business man and he was successful in his line, so Abby had said. And Bob was intellectual, for he was a poet. He had never had any of his poems published, he said, because he wanted to wait until he had a real contribution to make to modern literature. He made his living by trying to sell real estate. And Pat had been intellectual, but she did not appeal to me very greatly. Surely these two new ones would be different!

"And is Norman coming?" I asked, innocently.

"Heavens, no! He is good fun to play around with when we are out with his kind, but I wouldn't care to make a practice of having him come to the house. His reputation, I have found, isn't any too good."

Whose was? I wanted to ask, but I held my tongue. From what I had observed of life that week, cleanliness of thought and deed did not seem to be over-abundant.

When I was ready, Abby sprayed me from head to foot with the most delicate perfume that I had ever smelled. She stood away off from me so that only the daintiest suggestion of the sweet stuff would cling to my gown.

"If you don't break someone's heart tonight, it will

not be because you don't look perfectly adorable," declared Abby. "I'd give a lot to have been able to keep my innocent expression and my little-girl look about my eyes. You look at folks as if you trusted the whole world and found only gladness and joy and goodness in it."

I don't know how I looked at Abby when she said that, but I know I was amazed. Until a very short time ago, that is exactly how I felt towards the old world. I did trust folks. I was glad and happy and satisfied. But when I decided to have a career and found that I'd have to make a study of life, my eyes were so suddenly opened that I thought surely I revealed the shock that I felt. I was glad that I had not changed. Anyway, not too much. Oh, I wanted to look a little more worldly, a little less mountaineerish when I went back home, but I knew Mom and Dad would have regular fits and not want me to live in Charlotte in an apartment if I changed too much.

"Why, Abby!" was all that I said.

"I guess it is because you have always lived away off up in the mountains where there is so much beauty all around you. I used to hear folks say that you could take a person out of the mountains but you couldn't take the mountains out of the person. That is what must be wrong with you. You have something solid, something lovely, something beautiful from the old hills just naturally born in you. Take my advice and keep it. You are an exceptional girl. There are not any too many girls your age here in the city who don't smoke and drink and pet. I wish I had never started smoking. I wish I had never tasted wine. I wish we had never entered the set we run with. There! That's a big confession to make to you, Betsann, but I have been watching you even though I have taken you where I knew you'd see life as you thought you wanted to see it. I am glad you will get a slightly different slant of it tonight. At least, I hope everyone will stay sober."

"Thanks, Abby. I appreciate all you have said, though I can't exactly grasp it, every bit. But if Norman isn't coming, who will be your man?"

"Child, no one! My husband is away. I am a respectable married woman," laughingly Abby replied.

I don't know what sort of expression I wore. I hoped it wasn't as funny as it felt. But I was glad to hear Abby say she was a respectable married woman, for though at first I had thought that Norman was absolutely the most desirable male creature I had ever met, I had changed my mind.

Rust brought me a huge box of chocolates as a parting gift! Wasn't he just too thoughtful? Bob slipped a notebook to me when Pat wasn't looking. I had so wished she wouldn't come!

"It's some of my poems," he whispered. "In it there is one to you, but it isn't finished. I must speak to you alone this very night."

I was so excited! A poem to me and he wished to speak to me alone!

"Let's sit in the porch swing after a while," I suggested.

Pat came up to us then. "What are you two conspiring?" she asked, sweetly.

But before either of us could reply, they came. The girl—her name was Dorothea but they called her Dot—was the loveliest girl I have ever seen. She had hair that was as near like gold as anyone could want. It waved naturally from her low, broad brow and was coiled loosely on her neck. I determined then and there to let my hair grow out. After all, there isn't anything that makes a girl more attractive than her hair and with all these permanents that make each head look just like all the others, a girl with long hair like hers is certainly refreshing. She didn't wear much make-up, just a suggestion; and her lips were so artistically done that they looked positively natural. They may have been, too. She wore a dark blue, soft gown that made her blue eyes shine like stars. She was taller than I and was as straight as a sapling. Her teeth were so perfectly white and glistening that I glanced at her fingers to see if there was the tell-tale yellow. There was not! Well, I fell hard for her. But even though I longed to talk to her, to know her reactions about life, I was scared plumb stiff. She was so grand that I dared only stare dumbly at her.

And the man! Oh, how simply like a god he was! I had thought that Rust was handsome, but beside this new man Rust was common. Bob was a mere shadow beside him. His name was Terry Lane. Rust called him Terrible. Bob called him Lane. Dot called him Terry. When I stood beside him the top of my head came just to his chin. Oh, we didn't actually measure, but I made a mental note of it. His black hair—it was the blackest hair I have ever seen—was combed straight back, making his brow as white as marble. You'd never guess what color his eyes were. One was almost blue and one was almost brown! That was the first time I had ever seen eyes of two colors in one head. His nose was just right and there was the dearest dimple in his chin. Do you believe that dimples are caused by angels kissing babies? Terry wore white flannel trousers and a blue coat, white shirt and white and black shoes. I wished I had a legal question to ask him. I remembered that Rust's old store had threatened to take legal steps if I didn't pay their old bill, but I didn't want to ask Terry what sort of steps they could take.

Well, we sat around a little and talked. Then Rust shoved the furniture against the wall and tuned in on dance music and we danced. It was the first time for several days; so I had forgotten all I had learned. Rust danced with me first.

"I wish you would never go home," he murmured to me. "I wish you would stay here forever. You are the first girl I have ever known who dares to be herself with any sort of crowd."

I know I blushed. "I must go tomorrow," I said, simply.

Before he could say more, Bob cut in.

"This would be a grand time to slip out while they are all dancing," he suggested.

"All right. I'm not crazy about dancing anyway. It's too hot," I replied.

We were dancing towards the door when Terry took me away from Bob. "Loveliness, where have you always hid yourself?" asked Terry, swinging me away as easily as a mere child.

I was positively dumb. "Why—why, home!" I stammered.

He smiled and his whole face beamed. "Home, sweet home! That is the place for girls like you. When they come to the city, they become like all the others."

"Aren't all the others all right?" I asked, wondering what in the world to say.

"No, they have so little individuality. You have everything," he told me softly.

Goodness! "Oh, I think Dot is perfect," I managed to say.

"Dot is like you. She is different. She knows how to be herself wherever she goes. So do you. Don't you?" he asked, smiling right into my eyes.

I know my eyes were as big as saucers. They have a way of enlarging when I am excited or amazed. I was both then.

Well, he kept on talking to me through that dance and would not let anyone take me from him. Then dinner was ready. Who wanted to eat on such an occasion? I wasn't a bit hungry when we sat down, but Abby's cook was a perfect wonder, and I ate with a country appetite. It was a relief, too, not to have to worry about drinks. We had iced tea and that was positively all. Rust was on one side of me, Terry on the other. Each seemed determined to keep my plate filled! We had a lot of fun!

Bob managed to dance me out to the porch swing when we had finished eating. He wanted to hold my hand while he recited a poem that he was making about me, but I needed it to put a stray lock of hair in its place.

I did listen breathlessly, though.

"Dear Elizabeth, this has been a wonderful week to me. You have opened my eyes to a new kind of girl. I shall never be satisfied with the old kind again. You have awakened to my soul an ideal, and you will always be my ideal. You are beautiful, you are gentle, you are sweet and kind. And you are pure. Oh, I could adore you!" he exclaimed, pressing the palm of my hand to his lips! "Listen, Elizabeth, to these lines. They do not begin to express all my feelings, but I am not through with them yet."

Then he began from memory:

"Like deep and limpid pools, my dear,

Your eyes, so blue, so brave, so void of fear,

Fill me with awe, as star in skies—"

In a dark corner of the veranda someone sneezed! Bob jumped up, almost upsetting me. I was horrified. "Let's go inside, Elizabeth," said Bob icily.

My poem! I was so disappointed. We began to dance again. Soon Rust cut in on us. There was a look of mischief in his eyes as he danced me away from Bob.

"Bets, your eyes are like limpid pools of deep water," he murmured, in exactly the tone that Bob had used.

"That was you!" I stormed.

"Me, who? What?" he asked, innocently.

"I thought you were a gentleman, but gentlemen don't listen to other people's conversations," I told him.

"Bets, do you think I am going to stand by and let another fellow take my girl away from me? All is fair in love and war. It has been love this far, but it's going to be war if Bob doesn't behave. I found you first and you belong to me!"

"Is that so?" I demanded, still rather angry because he had spoiled my poem.

"Yes, it is so! Bets, don't you love me even a little bit?" he asked in an entirely different voice.

Did I? Why, I had never thought about loving anyone. Not even Jimmy! But before I could think up something to say, Terry took me away.

"Abby tells me you are leaving us tomorrow," he began at once.

"Yes, I must go back home in the morning," I replied, sorrowfully.

"If only I had known you were here all this week!"

Wasn't he going to be a bit intellectual? Did all the young men do the same kind of talking?

"I am sorry that you didn't know," I said, really truthfully.

Well, we just kept on with that sort of nonsense. And I had not even said half a dozen words to Dot. I had watched her and she had seemed a little more reserved than Pat. I didn't want to watch Pat. I'd never let her be one of my characters, unless I needed one that I didn't like myself.

About midnight we all sat down to rest and eat again. Abby passed sandwiches and punch, but it was fruit punch.

"I hope no one has missed anything stronger to-night," Abby said, smiling bewitchingly. "My little cousin doesn't approve of her generation drinking any-thing stronger than tea and milk, so I promised her to be a dry advocate tonight."

Her little cousin! I felt myself shrink. A queer feeling crept into my heart about Abby.

"I admire her spunk!" declared Terry. "I wish they all felt the same way. There would be less crime, less misery, fewer young men and girls coming before the courts. We've had a grand time tonight and we are all still sober. It's a shame that we have begun to feel that in order to have any fun we've got to be drunk."

"I am glad you let her have her way, Abby," added Dot. "You would be perfectly amazed at the sleepy-headed children that I sometimes have in my classes because they had been out till all hours the night be-fore and have had something to drink. They are not all boys, either. I feel sometimes as if I'd like to lay down the law, but I need to hold my job, and I keep still. Of course, when some of the teachers themselves are no better than the students, it is no wonder that they are going to the dogs at such a fast rate."

I felt my eyes get big.

"Why, the teachers don't drink, do they?" I asked.

"Not all of them, by any manner of means, but there are some who do. And not all the pupils are tough. We have a good many who are as seriously in earnest about their education as ever. It seems to me we have two extremes today. Those who are fine are very fine and those who are bad are rotten," Dot said.

Pat was the only one of us who was smoking. Her very eyes seemed like sparks of fire.

"We don't all have the same standard of morals," she said, slowly and very coolly.

"That is very true," Terry replied to her. "It is a good thing we don't, too, or there wouldn't be a decent man or woman left among us! We began to question the old standard after the War and found that some of the standards were a little too high for comfort. Therefore we began to lower them. They fell so fast and with such thumps that we have never succeeded yet in lifting some of them from the very mire itself. But if we are given time, I think we'll come to our senses and realize that after all, the world still needs decency and honor and purity in order to have citizens who are physically strong. If we kept on at the rate some are going, oldsters as well as youngsters, we would become a nation of physical weaklings. There aren't many of us here right now who can endure a day of physical labor such as our fathers and mothers once endured at our ages. We are softened. And we haven't been as dissipated as some of our contemporaries, either."

Well, Pat wilted and crushed out her cigarette. I was

listening with both ears and eyes. If only they would keep on talking! But they didn't. It was getting late—I mean, early—and they all had to work at something the next day; so they decided to go home.

As Bob left, he held my hand tight. "I'll mail that poem to you," he promised. "I'll never, never—"

"Bye, Bets! Hurry back. If you don't hurry, some of us will be coming out to your hills after you," Rust interrupted, as he deliberately snatched my hand from Bob. "Don't ever forget what I said to you. I'm not forgetting that you didn't answer me, too. Think about it and tell me next time!" he added very, very softly.

"You will come back?" asked Terry.

"I want to," I assured him.

"Please do. And when you do come, I want to know it immediately. Don't forget that. If you don't come—well, I'll search all over North Carolina till I find you!" and he squeezed my hand till it hurt.

Pat slipped out without a word!

"I should have enjoyed knowing you better, Elizabeth. I hope I may have the pleasure some day soon," was what Dot said to me.

Instantly an inspiration came to me! "Oh, do come out to the mountains and stay a whole week during your vacation!" I invited.

"That would be marvelous. Perhaps I can!"

Finally they were all gone. My last night in the city was over. On the morrow I was going back home.

I was glad!

Or was I? What about Libby Lou? What if she were

still there? Was she all that Jimmy had thought her earlier in the week? Was she like Pat or like Dot? Was she—well, was she a Christian? Then I wondered if I had really met a single Christian during the whole week that I had been in Charlotte. Finally I slept. I'd find out all I wanted to know when I reached home.

And I did! Oh, I did!

CHAPTER V

A S SOON as I was away from towns I drove slowly.
I wanted to think. I had seen so much of life during those few days. It was all a sort of jumble to me.
Rust, Bob, Terry, Patricia, Dorothea. And not in any
sense the least of all, Joe and Abby. Were they happy?
Were they getting from life all that it was possible to
get? What satisfaction did they have in getting drunk,
in spending so much money on things that lasted only
as long as it took to spend the money? We have so little
to spend on our rocky, hilly patch-farm that it hurt to
have them spend so lavishly, especially on just pleasures that were gone with the night.

I was not sure that I ever could appreciate that sort
of life. Yet, if I were with them all the time, perhaps
I should become so used to it all that I, too, would
soon be the biggest duck in the puddle, or the biggest
goose in the flock. I remembered that Jimmy said once
that we were fast becoming so used to many things we
once looked upon as sinful that they were no longer
considered wrong by most of the people. I guess it's
so. I didn't care so much that last night if my back and

arms were all exposed to anyone's view. I was used to being partially undressed by that time and I didn't care if the skirts were so tight that I could scarcely move. So I suppose I could get used to smoking cigarettes and even drinking—a very little.

Or could I?

I actually shuddered as I thought about it. But I decided it would be at least a year before I could even try life in my own apartment. If I should win the five hundred dollars, it would be as a mere grain of sand compared to what I should need, to live as these people lived. I had bought a writers' magazine. In it was the announcement of a book contest, a first novel contest. The prize was ten thousand dollars! Now that was something like it!

I had already decided that I'd begin my novel right away. With ten thousand dollars I could hope to start life as I wanted to. So I settled all these important questions, except to decide which of the three admirers I wanted to admire me most, for first it was one and then another, but I think I was finally decided upon Terry. I stepped on the gas and drove on as fast as I dared drive over the curves and up and down the hills.

Did you ever return from a trip feeling all inspired and determined to do something great and worthwhile? Then did you suddenly experience a terrific letdown and feel as if everything and everybody in the whole wide world were absolutely set against your ever becoming more than you were right that minute?

That is how I felt when I reached home. Mom had her head tied up. Cherry was nursing a bloody foot which had just been cut on a piece of glass. Dad was grieving over the loss of two young turkeys. There was not a single, solitary word from "Fragrant as Lilacs." No one seemed very thrilled because I was back, except that Mom did say she was glad I was home in time to cook supper!

We don't have dinner at supper time. It's breakfast, dinner, supper; and they all have to be substantial meals, too. Well, there was nothing for me to do except to remove my city clothes, slip into an old, faded print, and get busy.

Cherry hobbled into the kitchen and sat on a chair nibbling a cookie while I built a fire in the old wood cook stove.

"Libby Lou is just awful pretty," she told me so suddenly that I really did not quite understand her at first.

"Who?" I asked.

"Libby Lou! Marjorie's company. She's Jimmy's girl now!"

"Is that so? When did she leave?"

"She is still here. Oh, she is the beautifullest girl in the world! She is little and tiny and she looks like my Christmas doll with the golden curls and big blue eyes and red lips. She's only 'bout half as big as Jimmy."

"When is she going home?" I asked, carelessly.

"She's not going home. She's going to stay here forever and ever. Jimmy bought the old Miller place Wednesday. I guess they are going to get married and live in it," replied Cherry, apparently delighted.

I burned my finger on a hot stove lid and could have cried with the pain. So Jimmy had at last found his ideal girl. He *would* fall for a little thing. If she was as fragile as Cherry seemed to think, a lot of good she would be as a wife to a farmer in these rocky hills!

I heard a car stop.

"I'll bet that's Jimmy and Libby Lou!" cried Cherry, forgetting her injured foot as she ran from the kitchen.

I ran, too. In the opposite direction. I couldn't meet a stranger in the dress I was wearing. I decided to try to appear a little more as I intended to appear every day in my apartment.

When I reappeared, I wore a stunning pink linen that Abby had given me. I had even taken time to slip on white oxfords. My hair was still waved, for I had wanted to look unusually nice on Sunday at Sunday School—if I went. I knew I was quite presentable; so I felt no hesitancy as I went out on the front porch, where I heard voices.

Jimmy jumped up as I opened the door. He started towards me as he had always done, grabbing my hand and nearly shaking my arm loose. This time he hesitated. I think he must have realized that I was changed since I had spent a week in Charlotte. With considerable dignity he presented Libby Lou.

Cherry was right. She was perfectly beautiful but in an entirely different way from Dorothea or any girl I had seen in Charlotte. She was small. She was like a doll. She was graciously sweet, and it wasn't an affected pose. It was natural. I felt myself wilt. I just knew she knew I had posed!

"We are on our way to a party at Garry's, Betsann. We stopped by for you," Jimmy explained, after we had exchanged the first greetings and introductions.

"Thanks, Jimmy, but I am simply too dead for sleep to go to a party tonight. I have been up till morning hours every single night since I have been away and have been dancing and dining and gadding till I must snatch some sleep tonight," I boasted. "It is sweet of you, though, to stop for me."

Poor Jimmy! I may have imagined it, but it seemed to me that he looked at me a little harder when I said I had been dancing. I am sure he must have thought I was perfectly hopeless now. They coaxed, but I was adamant. So they left without me.

I finished supper as I was and called Mom and Dad. Did they praise Libby Lou!

"She is one of the finest little girls I have ever seen," Dad said. "If Jimmy does win her, he will be a lucky boy. If I had a son, I'd be proud to have him marry Libby Lou. She will make him a good, true, capable wife."

"She is pretty, too. She will never let herself be slouchy and untidy about her house. I know she will be a good housekeeper," Mom added. "She is little, I know, but sometimes these little girls can turn out more work than the larger ones. They seem to be all energy."

"Are they really engaged?" I managed to ask, and I

hope I asked it naturally. Why shouldn't I, though? Jimmy was nothing special to me!

"No one seems to know for certain," Mom said. "Jimmy has bought the old Miller place and has begun to fix it up, but so far no one has said they were actually going to get married."

"I hope she plays and sings at Sunday School in the morning," Cherry contributed. "Betsann, she can make our organ just talk. And she sings so sweet. I hope I can sing like that when I get big."

"I am glad you are home, Betsann. I hope you will see as much of her as you can. I don't know how long she is going to stay, but she is one girl I want you to know better," Mom told me.

"Well," I murmured. "I'll see as much of her as I have time to. If I begin to pick cotton for Dad next week and try to begin a novel I want to write, I'll not have much time to see anyone."

"Suppose you bring her home for dinner tomorrow from Sunday School. Bring Marjorie and Jimmy, too. Dad can kill that old rooster and I'll make some dumplings," Mom suggested.

"Well, if I go," I consented.

"If you go!" exclaimed Cherry. "Why, you always go, and Libby Lou is going to teach my class."

"I am not in your class," I reminded the child.

If those Charlotte dinners had been long, this supper seemed endless. Finally it was over, the dishes washed, and all the evening chores were done. I said I was tired and went to bed soon.

But not to sleep!

I had too much to think about. Libby Lou and her numerous splendid, super-fine qualities; Jimmy and how grand he looked in his new gray summer suit, and how he looked at me; and the Charlotte bunch. Finally, I decided I was tired enough to stay in bed the next morning instead of going to Sunday School. I turned over again and tried to sleep. But I became positively wide-awake. Suddenly I remembered that I did not know a thing about the Sunday School lesson and I might change my mind. I got up, lighted the lamp, and read the lesson in my quarterly. As I read I became sleepy, and as soon as I got back to bed, I went to sleep.

Of course, I did go to Sunday School. I wore a ravishing white swiss with red dots, a red velvet sash, a perky red felt hat, and white shoes. It was a last summer outfit of Abby's, but it was new to me and all the rest of my home crowd. Even Cherry had eyes for me when I was all ready.

Libby Lou was in very simple white. Jimmy wore his new gray suit. He had acquired more poise and dignity during my absence.

"Betsann, Libby Lou is going to sing a special song for us. Will you play it for her?" asked Jimmy.

"If I can," I replied.

It was a new song to me, but I managed to play it. It was time to begin before she had time to sing it, though.

"Cherry said you play beautifully. Won't you play

for us this morning?" I asked, just as sweetly as I could.

She certainly could play! Never had our old organ sounded so full of music. Just before we went to our classes, she sang. I had distinguished her voice during the congregational songs, but I was not really prepared for the quality that she displayed as she sang alone. There was a depth, a warmth, a feeling that made tears come to my eyes. She sang with perfect ease and it sounded as if she meant every word of the song.

"Once far from God and dead in sin,
No light my heart could see;
But in God's Word the Light I found,
Now Christ liveth in me.

"With longing all my heart is filled,
That like Him I may be,
As on the wondrous thought I dwell
That Christ liveth in me.

"Christ liveth in me, Christ liveth in me,
Oh! what a salvation is this,
That Christ liveth in me."

If ever Christ did live in a girl, He certainly must have been living in Libby Lou. No wonder Jimmy was crazy about her. She was the sort who had "the listening heart" that he told me about once.

A comforting thought came to me. She would have

a good influence over Cherry and the other children, and Mom wouldn't miss me so much if they lived in the Miller place, not far from our house! Libby Lou would be a sweet neighbor! Perhaps I could make out with the five hundred dollars at first. I did not want to live so extravagantly until I had really made a name and a place for myself in the literary world. Then I could go sooner!

Libby Lou's class was near enough to mine so that I could hear her as she taught the children. In our little one-room church all the classes are taught in the same room. Libby Lou had a soft voice, but it was penetrating, too.

During the closing exercises she made a little talk. Never had I heard such a talk! On the little old blackboard she had drawn a picture of three roads. One went straight till it branched and became two roads. The first was called "The Little Children's Road." The road that led upward and ended in heaven was called "Jesus' Road." The other that led down and ended in hell was called "Satan's Road." She had drawn some little figures in each one to represent the boys and girls and men and women who were traveling in each road. As she explained the drawing, she said all the very young children who did not yet know the difference between right and wrong and were not old enough to decide definitely that they wanted to be Christians were safe in The Little Children's Road. There came a time, however, in every child's life when he must stand face to face with the cross (she had drawn a cross at the entrance of the two cross roads) and must decide for himself which road he would follow. If the child accepted the Lord Jesus for his Saviour, confessing his sins and repenting, he started up the Jesus Road and the Lord Jesus Himself would lead him all the way by sending the Holy Spirit to abide in his heart and direct his paths. But if the child put off the day of decision and did not accept Christ as his Saviour, he started down Satan's Road with Satan himself as his leader! Everyone in the church was walking in one or the other of the three roads. In which were we?

In which was I?

You may be very sure I didn't like to face the fact that I was already walking in Satan's Road and was headed towards hell—if there is a hell. Sometimes I am inclined to think there isn't. Why would God create man and then send him to hell? Cherry had to learn a verse that said, "God is love." Well, if God is love, how could love send a soul to hell for eternity? It was too much for me to fathom. I had an uncomfortable feeling when I was so plainly told that I was headed for hell. I didn't like it! I did not like to be told about it, either.

Then she gave the invitation to anyone who wanted to start up Jesus' Road that morning to come up and sit on the front bench. After the Sunday School was dismissed Jimmy and she would pray with all who came. Cherry was the very first one up there! My very own sweet little sister! I'll confess that I fuss about her a lot, but I know she is good. In all her nine years she never did a bad thing that I know about. She had been mischievous and full of pranks and fun, but she has been honest, pure, and sweet. The idea of thinking that a child like her was lost! I felt like getting up and taking her right home. Well, some other children came. There were four others, all older than Cherry, all from Libby Lou's class. I suppose she had prepared them for her talk. She was lovely about it, I'll have to say that much for her. She did not urge the children and she put the facts plain. She quoted her Bible for all she said. I don't know mine well enough to be able to tell you the verses, but I did jot down a reference or two. There were John 3:16, John 10:28, John 1:12, John 3:7, John 14:6. John must have a lot of verses about salvation! When I get time, I'll read the whole book of John.

While Libby Lou was talking, Jimmy sat with his head bowed, as if he were praying. When he did look up, he looked right squarely at me, and I never in all my life saw such a pleading look. I turned my head and glanced out the window. I was not ready to give up life and everything just when I was beginning to live and study life so that I could write all about it. I simply would have to stay in Satan's Road a while longer. Some day I might decide to change roads, but not that day!

I went outside and talked with folks while Libby Lou and Jimmy talked and prayed with the children. When they did come out, Libby Lou's face was simply glowing. Cherry ran over to me and hugged me.

"I am a Christian, Betsann. I am going in Jesus' Road. You are a Christian, too. Aren't you, Sis?" she asked, her eyes shining.

"Let's not talk about it now, darling," I replied.

Then I immediately wished I hadn't said it. The light seemed to fade in her eyes and her smile changed. She seemed disappointed all over.

"Well," she said. "I guess Mom will want to know, though."

"Oh, yes, be sure to tell Mom," I said, trying to encourage her.

We did have a delightful day. Libby Lou was as full of fun as she was of piety. When she laughed, it was contagious, for she laughed all over, as if she enjoyed laughing. It wasn't a loud, boisterous laugh. It was as musical as any laugh could be. But it was fun to laugh with her. Jimmy seemed as proud of her as an old gobbler. She seemed deeply interested in my writing. She even said she wished she could put her thoughts down on paper, but she didn't suppose she could be still long enough to write more than three pages at a time. That was as long as any letter she had ever written. She had read a lot, but books that I had never heard of and magazines I didn't know existed. Then she explained that a good many of the books were religious novels and Bible study books; and the magazines were religious magazines that contained stories as well as explanations of the signs of the times and how prophecies were being fulfilled and just lots of things.

"Do you believe the Lord is coming soon?" she asked me.

Why, I had never given it a thought!

"I am sure I don't know what to believe," I replied honestly.

"I wish I had some of my magazines with me so you could read them. It is more thrilling than any fiction to read about how the prophecies are being fulfilled. I simply devour all I can find about the conditions in Europe and all over the world. Even America is revealing the great truth. Oh, it is wonderful, and I do believe with all my heart that He is coming soon."

I shuddered. I don't want Him to come soon. I want my career a while first.

"What will happen when He comes?" I asked, for I was really scared.

"You will find all about in it First Thessalonians, the fourth chapter and the last three verses. I think I know it by heart. 'For the Lord Himself shall descend from heaven with a shout, with the voice of the archangel, and with the trump of God: and the dead in Christ shall rise first: Then we which are alive and remain shall be caught up together with them in the clouds, to meet the Lord in the air: and so shall we ever be with the Lord. Wherefore comfort one another with these words.'

"Comfort one another!" Indeed, it was no comfort to me.

"I want Him to come soon, but I do hope some who

are dear to me will be saved before He comes," Jimmy said softly.

I wondered who they were. His mother and father and Marjorie and his sisters and brothers are all Christians. They are the most faithful family in all our community. Not a one ever misses church and Sunday School unless sickness prevents their going.

"I believe He is coming soon," Marjorie said. "I hope that He does, for it will put an end to the suffering and sorrows of thousands of Christians. And yet even if He does wait for many years we need not feel afraid or forsaken. We know that He is preparing a place for us, and that He will come and receive us unto Himself. When I think of the wars and greed and hatred that fill the world I shudder, until I remember what Jesus said: 'Peace I leave with you; my peace I give unto you . . . Let not your heart be troubled, neither let it be afraid.' And those words of Isaiah: 'Thou wilt keep him in perfect peace, whose mind is stayed on thee.' Isn't it wonderful to know that He will be with us till the end of the world? How I pity those who have turned their backs upon Jesus! How much they miss in life, and how much they will miss in the life to come."

I was one who had turned her back upon Jesus. I was the most uncomfortable person in the world while Marjorie was talking. In my heart I knew that she was right, but I wouldn't admit it. I still wanted my career more than anything else.

Well, I was glad when the subject was changed. Soon it was time for young people's meeting at the church and Libby Lou and her host and hostess were going to attend.

"Aren't you coming along?" asked Jimmy, surprise and disappointment in his voice and expression.

"Not this time. I am tired," I begged off.

"Don't you feel well?" he asked, searching my face.

"Oh, yes, but I am just plain worn out and I have a hard week ahead of me," I said.

"Do you want me to stay here with you?" he asked, something queer in his tones.

"Indeed, no! I'm going to bed by dark. You go on with the girls," I urged.

I didn't want anybody! I had too much on my mind. I never had been in such a "picklement," as old Tom says. I was glad the next day was Monday and that Dad had promised me cash for my cotton picking. I intended to work hard so that I'd have another payment on my typewriter in two weeks anyway. As I picked the fluffy, white stuff, I expected to plan my novel. In that way I wouldn't be wasting my time.

But, oh dear, it's so hard to make one's mind do just as she wants it to. That cotton picking week was a lot different from what I had anticipated.

CHAPTER VI

I DREAMED and dreamed the whole night. I just know I did, for I dreamed so many dreams. I don't care what science says!

First I dreamed that I was dead and that I was being wafted up and up and up, as I've seen leaves and birds going up and up into the sky, without making any effort. It was a most exquisite sensation. As I got farther and farther up, I began to hear music. I simply cannot describe it, for it was too wonderful for human description. Voices soon joined the instruments and I recognized children's voices among the others. I do not remember any of the words, but I knew they were hymns of praise. Then a light began to glow, at first softly radiant. As I was borne nearer, the light increased in brightness, but it still was bearable. Suddenly before me was a gleaming golden gate.

"Who shall ascend into the hill of the Lord? or who shall stand in His holy place? He that hath clean hands and a pure heart; who hath not lifted up his soul unto vanity, nor sworn deceitfully. He shall receive the blessing from the Lord, and righteousness from the God of his salvation," a voice clear and distinct came to me.

I stood perfectly still. I don't know what I stood on, but I know I stood. I suddenly became conscious of the awful fact that those beautiful gates would not open for me. Then I began to drop, slowly, slowly, slowly, but very surely. The light faded. No longer did I hear the music. No longer could I smell the fragrance of flowers. Then I awoke. How thankful I was that I awoke before I began to descend!

Finally I went to sleep again, and dreamed I heard a shout, a shout of victory, and I looked upward. There was a great, gleaming, growing light from the East. I realized what was happening. The Lord was descending in the clouds! I saw forms all around me, forms that were ascending to meet Him in the air just as Libby Lou had said. At first I did not recognize anyone. Then I saw Mom, Cherry, my Dad, Jimmy close to Libby Lou and Marjorie. I could look no longer. I was being left! It seemed to me that my heart simply would burst. I felt smothered, suffocated, sick. Again a voice spoke and I heard these words, "He that believeth on the Son hath everlasting life: and he that believeth not the Son shall not see life; but the wrath of God abideth on him." I awoke as I fell upon my face.

I felt utterly weak and exhausted. I felt condemned. Here was I, a good girl, an obedient daughter, a faithful attendant at Sunday School and church, yet I was being left. The gates of heaven would not open for me. Was it just because I wouldn't surrender everything to the Lord? I believed in Him with my head.

Why, everyone in our settlement believes there is a God, believes that Jesus died to save the world. We know that to be a fact. Something was wrong!

As I lay there, perfectly miserable, I thought of our old silver spoons. They have been in use for so long that the silver plate has worn off. And that was exactly the way I felt as I came home from Charlotte! The nearer home I drove, the more deeply I got into the hills with their green and everlasting mountains, the more tarnished I felt! I did everything I could to put the feeling away from me, for I had done nothing so terrible during the week. I hadn't drunk a drop of liquor. I hadn't taken a single puff of a cigarette. I hadn't let Rust kiss me when he had wanted to. But I knew as I lay there so wide awake that I was tarnished in God's sight. What was I to do?

It was too late now to go back on my plans. I had bragged too much about how I was going to become a great writer and how I was studying life and a whole lot of stuff like that. I simply could not endure staying home and having Jimmy and Libby Lou right there in the Miller place. Not that Jimmy meant anything special to me! It just gave me a queer, sickening feeling, that was all. Well, finally I slept again. I dreamed and dreamed, dreamed I was back in Charlotte, dreamed I had written my novel and that it had won the ten thousand dollars. I don't know what all I did dream! Then I heard Dad call me.

Isn't it a good thing that a perfectly new, bright sunny morning brings with it a freshness of spirit and a renewed determination, that the dreads and fears we have in the darkness of night are largely vanished? After I had been up a while I ate breakfast. At first I didn't feel as if I could swallow a bite, but Mom's biscuits and butter and honey and bran and cream are irresistible. I began to feel more nearly normal and was ready for the cotton picking as soon as Dad himself.

When I pick cotton I put on a pair of Dad's overalls, which I have to roll way up because they are too long for me. Then I wear an old shirt with long sleeves, tie a handkerchief around my neck, and top it off with either a sunbonnet or a big, floppy hat. We forget looks when we pick cotton.

Nothing tremendously important happened on Monday till Billy brought the mail. Bob had sent me his poem! It was perfectly gorgeous, six stanzas, and the last two contained a declaration of his love for me, also a statement that he could not live without me, for I was his inspiration, his life, his all in all! Whee! I sank down beneath the shade of a big peach tree and re-read it all. My first actual proposal on paper! I was awfully excited. But I didn't want anyone to know it yet. I was not absolutely sure how I felt about him. I liked him a lot—until Terry came. Then! Well, I wasn't sure.

I forgot my plot for my novel, I forgot my perplexities of the day before, I forgot everything except that I was loved! I slept better that night.

Tuesday I was dressed as on Monday, except that my garb was soiled by that day, for picking cotton is hot work. Billy brought me another letter! It was not a poem. At least it wasn't in rhyme. But to me it was positively the most thrilling, the most satisfying, the most delightful letter that ever I had received: I haven't let a soul see it, of course, but this is what it said:

"Darling!" it began. "How long the hours are! How dull the sun is! How empty my life is! Why? you are gone! During all my life, I have been expecting you. Then you came, but for so short a moment. I hardly realized it was you at first, but as I watched you and studied you, my heart and my head told me you were the girl. Where are you, my precious one? Abby gave me your address, but how does one reach you? Is it too far to drive in an evening? If I were not forced to go out of town over Sunday, I would reach you if I had to wade water and climb hills. When will you come back to Charlotte? When, when! That is the cry of my heart, for you are the answer to all my longings, to all my ambitions, to all my ideals. As Marcus loved Lygia, so do I love you!

"Please believe me,

"Terry."

Isn't that a perfectly beautiful letter? But who was Marcus and who was Lygia and how did he love her? How dumb I am! How could a young, rising lawyer, a man of the world, who saw girls and girls and girls, find all this in me? Well, Bob's poem vanished from my mind. I knew the answer to his proposal. I was sorry, for I could not bear to hurt any one, especially one who loved me. But I did not love Bob! I was all a-flutter as I went back to my cotton picking, the letter in the breast pocket of my shirt.

I had hardly started again when Libby Lou and Jimmy arrived. Jimmy looked quite natural, for he was in his old overalls and work shirt again. Libby Lou had on a darling pink print. It was as fresh and crisp as a pink hollyhock with the morning dew still on it.

"Betsann, Marjorie is going to have a party tomorrow night and she sent a special invite to you. She said for you to be sure to come," Jimmy said, picking cotton and stuffing it into my pick sack.

"Well, if I'm not too tired, I'll come," I replied.

"Do you care if I come in the morning and help you pick?" asked Libby Lou. "We don't have much cotton around Asheville and I never did pick any till I came here. I'd love to pick a whole day right along with you so that I could go back home and say I'd picked cotton all day."

Go back home!

"I'd love to have you, but your back would feel as if it were broken by evening and you wouldn't enjoy the party very much," I warned her.

But she came! She was too cunning for words, for she wore a pair of Jimmy's overalls that swallowed her more completely than Dad's does me. But she didn't seem to mind how we laughed. She meant business. She stayed right with me for more than two hours. When she began to lag a little, we rested.

"Do you like this part of the country?" I asked, as we sat beneath the big old walnut tree.

"Oh, I love it. It is so different from Asheville. I'd love to live here all the time," she told me smilingly.

"Maybe you will," I ventured.

She blushed. "I'm afraid not," was all she said, and I felt rather rebuked.

"Isn't Marjorie a dear?" I asked, thinking I might lead her on.

"Marjorie is simply precious," Libby Lou declared with enthusiasm. "I think Jimmy is, too! He is one of the finest young men I have ever known. In fact, I think the whole family is exceptionally grand."

Well, evidently she liked her in-laws!

"Every one up here thinks the Caspers are just about the best ever," I quickly assured her.

Then we talked some more about the perfect Caspers. Presently we started picking again. I had longed to tell her about Bob's poem and about Terry's letter, but I just couldn't do it. I did decide that I would tell Marjorie about them at the party, and she could get the good news across to Jimmy. In that way he would learn that some one had found in me his ideal girl, even as he had found his in Libby Lou.

Since Dad insisted that we quit early, I didn't get my hundred pounds picked. We all thought that Libby Lou had done well in picking sixty-three pounds. Dad wanted to pay her, but she just laughed at him and refused to be paid.

"Why, it was fun!" she cried. "Oh, I guess if I had

to do it day in and day out, I might not think it was so much fun, but a day of it was heaps of fun. It is such clean, fluffy, beautiful stuff. It made me think of something very pure and sinless, a lovely baby or a young person who lives every day in such a way that his every word and deed is done so as to glorify the Lord Jesus."

"This is pretty now," Dad replied. "After it frosts and the cotton is stained, it isn't so pretty."

"Neither is life so pretty after sin has entered it. Isn't it funny how the Lord can speak to us in everything, even in cotton?" she asked, smiling wistfully.

Cherry drank in every word. I was silent. Oh, I was listening, but I simply didn't have anything to say. I was afraid I had some stains in my life!

"Libby Lou, I'm like the cotton now. Ain't I?" asked Cherry, hugging the girl.

"Indeed you are, darling. Your sins have been washed as white as snow," she assured her, kissing her.

Cherry's sins! The very idea! What did that child know about sins? She has been a perfect pupil at school. She has gone to Sunday School ever since Mom had to carry her there. She has always told the truth since Mom caught her in a story about going into June's watermelon patch with three other little girls who were older than she was. She is simply a dear, sweet, innocent child. And Libby Lou was talking about her sins having been forgiven!

Why, even I wasn't so bad! I can't think of a single very bad thing in my life, unless it is that I get angry and say mean, hateful things about some of the neighbors sometimes. I don't tattle as much as some of them do, and I never repeat anything one says about the other unless I am dead sure it is the truth. I haven't surrendered my heart and life to the Lord Jesus, yet, but He knows I mean to do so before I die.

All this had made me forget Terry's letter, but as soon as Libby Lou was gone and I was undressing, so as to get ready for the party, I felt a piece of paper in my shirt pocket, and there was the precious letter. Everything dark turned resplendent then.

I dressed with meticulous care. (I am learning how to use new words!) I wore a stunning half-evening gown that was too small for Abby and that didn't lack very much of being too small for me. It was yellow organdy. Bob had said it made him think of moonlight. I wondered what it would do to Jimmy. It took me a long time to do my hair, as cotton picking is rather disastrous to waves. But finally I was ready.

"My, Sis, you look as beautiful as Libby Lou!" exclaimed Cherry. "I didn't know you were so pretty."

You just don't know how those few words helped me. I kissed her and hurried off to the party. I was the most dressed up girl there! It made me feel rather conspicuous. I should have known that I should wear simply a voile or a pretty print. It's always understood that we dress for fun when we go to parties. Even Libby Lou wore very simple blue linen. Marjorie had on a white dimity with brown polka dots. And there I was in a frilly yellow organdy dress, sleeveless, low in the back, though not actually backless, and too long for out-door games that we played in the moonlight. I had to grab my tight skirts every time I ran, and I did play, for I couldn't be a wallflower on that night. Once I tripped and Jimmy caught me. He held me dreadfully tight for a second. I guess he was afraid I'd actually fall.

"You look pretty sweet, Betsann," he whispered to me.

"Thanks," I replied, coolly.

That was no way for him to treat Libby Lou.

I had a good chance to tell Marjorie about Bob's poem and a wee, little suggestion about Terry's letter. Of course, I mentioned Rust, too, though he had faded somewhat in the background with Bob. She was awfully interested and thought it was great. She told me that Libby Lou was engaged and was to be married soon! I was about to find out some more when we were interrupted. I didn't get to say another word to her privately.

Every one, almost every one, had a grand time. How different it all was to what we had done in Charlotte. We played games in the moonlight till our sides ached from laughing. Then we sat around on the porch and in the yard and sang. One of the boys had his fiddle with him and another had brought his banjo. Jimmy got his guitar out and they all played to our singing. My, but it was pretty! Then we ate home-made ice cream and chocolate cake. We dispersed for our homes around eleven, for we all had some sort of work to do the next day. Jimmy, Marjorie, and Libby Lou walked home with me. We live less than a mile apart. I guess I was too tired to sleep, for I didn't sleep very well.

The rest of the week was quite uneventful. I saw no more of any of the Caspers or their guest. I picked cotton like a good picker. I forgot my novel. Somehow I couldn't plan a plot and pick cotton, too. I seldom waited for Billy to leave the mail. I was right there at the box to receive what he had to leave. But not a day did he give me a single word from "Fragrant as Lilacs." That was something else that had begun to worry me. Then I'd get out the card and re-read the statement that if the story were not found available, it would be returned soon. It had been weeks and weeks since I had received that card. Surely they had found my story available!

By Saturday evening I had over five dollars coming to me. In another week, if it didn't rain, I'd have enough to take to Charlotte to make at least a ten dollar payment. I didn't suppose they would object if it were not fifteen again.

Sunday morning it rained, a perfectly grand rain that looked as if it would last the whole day. I was glad to see it. I was tired. And I dreaded going to Sunday School and having Libby Lou or Jimmy or some other "preacher" remind me that I was lost! Sunday afternoon the clouds disappeared and it was a glorious evening. Cherry begged and begged me to take her to the young people's meeting. She had missed Sunday School, too, and had not seen Libby Lou all day.

I went, but I wished I had stayed home. The lesson

was on consecration and faith. We learned that through Christ we could do all things. We learned what others had done through faith. There were George Mueller and his orphanage in England, Judson and his wife, Ann, Dwight L. Moody, and others that I had never heard of. They had lived for Jesus only. Then Libby Lou "brought a message in song." But before she did that, she brought one in plain words.

"We have had a wonderful lesson on faith and consecration," she said. "Because it taught us about those who have lived instead of those who are living, we may be a little inclined to think that perhaps God does not need lives consecrated to Him now as He has needed them in the past. If we do have that idea, we are mistaken. He needs young people now who will completely dedicate their lives to Him, even as young Dwight L. Moody did, and let Him show the world today what He can still do with a girl or a boy whose life is centered in the Lord Jesus. As I sing, will you please turn to the song and read the words to yourselves, asking yourselves the questions? Oh, I long to see you young people completely surrendered to your Saviour!"

"Wait just a minute, please," Jimmy interrupted me as I started to play. "As Libby Lou sings this song, if there are those who will stand up here with me and say along with me, for I say it from the depths of my heart, 'Lord Jesus, I want to be wholly Thine. I want to live day by day only as Thou wouldst have me live,' please come. All right, girls!"

How glad I was that I was playing! Of course, I

couldn't do anything but sit still—even if I had been ready to give up my career and everything for Jesus.

The song goes like this:

"*Jesus is standing in Pilate's hall—*
Friendless, forsaken, betrayed by all;
Hearken! what meaneth the sudden call!
What will you do with Jesus?

"*Jesus is standing on trial still,*
You can be false to Him if you will,
You can be faithful thro' good or ill;
What will you do with Jesus?

"*Will you evade Him as Pilate tried?*
Or will you choose Him, whate'er betide?
Vainly you struggle from Him to hide;
What will you do with Jesus?

"*Will you, like Peter, your Lord deny?*
Or will you scorn from His foes to fly,
Daring for Jesus to live or die?
What will you do with Jesus?

"*'Jesus, I give Thee my heart today!*
Jesus, I'll follow Thee all the way,
Gladly obeying Thee!' will you say,
'This will I do with Jesus!'

"*What will you do with Jesus?*
Neutral you cannot be;
Some day your heart will be asking,
'What will He do with me?'"

I've copied it all because she sang it all and I had to play it all. I never felt so terrible in my life. My eyes burned with tears. I swallowed them back, because I just would not be emotional! There was something in Libby Lou's voice that would melt a heart of stone, and mine wasn't stone yet. Of course, nearly every one who was a Christian at all was standing beside Jimmy. When the song ended, he waited a minute.

"Is there any one else?" he asked, softly, and I could just feel him looking at me. I sat still!

"Mr. Woodward, please dismiss us," Jimmy said, with a sadness in his voice that was distressing. He should have been glad, for he must have succeeded in what he was trying to do.

Well, during the week I heard that Libby Lou had gone home to get ready for her wedding. I picked cotton and worked hard. At least every other day there was a letter from Terry. Bob never answered the one I wrote him. Rust wrote once, just a friendly, newsy letter, urging me to hurry back to Charlotte. The letters helped me a lot. For some reason I wasn't feeling any too well. I lost my appetite. Mom said I was working too hard and wanted me to pick shorter hours, but I was anxious to go to Charlotte.

"Betsann, your mother and I have decided to pay you in advance so that you will have ten dollars by Friday night and you may spend the week-end in Charlotte. You're working too hard, but you won't stop. Maybe this will stop you," Dad said on Thursday night.

Hurrah! I'd see Terry! I wouldn't have to go to

church Sunday, and I wouldn't see the superintendent of the Sunday School!

"You needn't come back before Tuesday, Betsann. I want the car on Wednesday, or you could spend the week with Abby," Dad said, as I was ready to start on Saturday morning.

"It will be all right, Dad. I'll be ready to come back by Tuesday," I said, too happy for words.

But I didn't wait till Tuesday!

CHAPTER VII

SINCE I was anxious to have as much time as possible in Charlotte, I started early on Saturday morning. As I was driving happily along about two miles from home, I saw a familiar figure ahead of me. I stopped.

"Want a ride?" I asked.

I wished later that I had waved and had driven on!

"Going far, Betsann?" asked Jimmy, sitting beside me.

Jimmy looked positively sick. Libby Lou had been gone only a few days, but here was Jimmy looking as if he had lost his best friend and was just returning from the funeral.

"I'm on my way to Charlotte," I managed to reply quite naturally.

"Will you be gone long?" he asked, without glancing at me at all.

"Not a whole week this time, for Dad wants the car. But I am looking forward to a big time while I am there."

"You had a big time before. Didn't you, Bets?" he asked, rather far-offish.

93

"I certainly did. I met some perfectly grand people and was entertained as if I were already a celebrity. I danced in the best places, dined in the most fashionable eating establishments in the city, went to picture shows, to a concert, and had dinner in a grand apartment. Then the last night, Abby gave a dinner-dance in my honor, and Jimmy, I met *the* man!" I simply had to tell it!

"You did? I hope he is all you deserve," he muttered.

"Oh, he is! He is a lawyer, and is he smart! He has high ideals and knows life as I want to know it so that I can write about it," I bragged.

"Most lawyers are smart," he remarked. "Is he a Christian?"

"A Christian? How do I know? I am sure I did not ask him."

Of all the questions to ask!

"It might be well for you to find you. The Bible says, 'Be ye not unequally yoked together with unbelievers: for what fellowship hath righteousness with unrighteousness? and what communion hath light with darkness?' So Betsann, I want to see you in partnership with a Christian," Jimmy declared.

"But, don't you see, silly, that it would not be obeying the Bible? What right would a Christian have to become my partner, as you call it? I am not a Christian!" I reminded him.

"You may not be a Christian now, but you are going to be one soon. I am still praying for you. Marjorie prays for you every day. Libby Lou promised that she would pray for you every day until you are saved. We all know that God hears and answers prayers and we know that 'Prayer changes things.' Prayer can change hearts. Prayer can change lives. So we are all expecting you to become a Christian very soon," he replied, oh, so seriously.

I felt dreadfully uncomfortable.

"It's thoughtful of you all, I am sure. But you should not put yourselves to so much bother, especially when each of you has so much to think of now with the wedding coming on and everything," I said.

"Your becoming a Christian is the most important thing I know of right now, Betsann," he said.

How would Libby Lou have liked that!

"Well, as I have said before, I expect to be a Christian some day. And I'm not so bad anyway. I've never done any great crime. Why should you all be praying so hard for me as if I were the most terrible sinner in all our community? Seems to me you might better be praying about some of these liquor men, since you are so set against liquor," I remembered suddenly.

"Aren't you set against liquor any more?" he wanted to know, looking hard at me for the first time.

"Why, certainly, and yet while I was in Charlotte I saw some of the city's very best people drinking. Some of them even got drunk. I saw young society girls drinking strong wines and then I saw them tipsy. I saw girls and women smoking right along with the men.

Jimmy, I saw life while I was in the city!" I tried to impress him with these facts.

"Did you enjoy that life, Betsann? Did it make you feel as if you were a better girl because you had been where women and girls were drinking and smoking? Did it make you feel proud of them and proud that you were among them? Did you feel as if the Lord Jesus would be found sitting beside any of them, drinking with them, or smoking with them? Would you have asked Him to be your partner in dancing? I need not ask you if you drank, too, for I know that you did not. Neither did you smoke. You are just naturally too fine a girl to have fallen quite so low. Your mother is too fine a woman to have a daughter who would have succumbed to the temptations about her. I know, down deep in your heart, it was disgusting to you. Am I right?" suddenly asked Jimmy, turning squarely toward me.

I hate a liar. I hate a lie. I simply have never made a practice of lying, no matter in what corner I was placed. But this was one time that I was sorely tempted to lie. Jimmy was right! I was too hard-headed, too stubborn to want him to know he was right. But I had to acknowledge it.

"Well," I said slowly. "I'll have to confess that I have been places where I felt more comfortable and less ill at ease."

"Oh, Betsann, please don't trifle with sin. Please don't compromise with Satan. It is not like you to go half way with anything. I dread to have you go to Charlotte and mix with that crowd at all. Why don't you mail in your payments?" he asked.

Mail in my payments! Of all things! Miss seeing Terry? I had to remind myself again of Terry, for Jimmy was getting me all upset.

"I prefer taking my payments myself," I replied, stiffly.

"I suppose you do. What are you writing now?" he changed the subject, and I was wondering if he were going all the way with me!

"I've been picking cotton, Jimmy. How could I write and pick cotton, too?" I asked, trying to hide my real feelings.

"I just wondered. Libby Lou thought you were a really intelligent girl, and able to write good stories. She admired you lots," he told me, and I may have imagined he spoke very tenderly of Libby Lou.

"Did she? Well, she was a marvelous story teller. She should try writing, herself," I replied, honestly.

"Bets, she is the sort of Christian that I wish you were. She has an every-day religion, for she is every day of the week just what she is on Sunday. There is no put-on and take-off about it. It's the sort that fills her whole life with cheer and happiness and usefulness. She is the same on a rainy Thursday as she is on a sunny Tuesday. She is the same when she is deeply troubled about something as when she is gay and happy. It's all because she really loves the Lord and has thoroughly consecrated her whole life to Him. She would like to be a foreign missionary, but she is not robust enough for foreign work. She says there is a real need for Christian service at home as well as on foreign fields. She sees the need and does her best to fill it. Stop there at Cooper's mail box, Bets. I'll get out there," he added, as we drew near that spot, which was really a secluded, shady spot.

"Libby Lou must be a girl with a listening heart, Jimmy," I said, mildly. My throat was dry. I was angry, hurt, sick, and I couldn't figure out exactly why.

There had been a time when Jimmy had thought I was pretty fine, myself. But that was before he got so pious and before he met Libby Lou. It certainly did change Jimmy to get so deep in religion.

"Yes, I do believe she has a listening heart, Bets. I believe she tries to hear the Lord say to her, 'This is the way. Walk ye in it.' That's what I wish for you, for after all is said and done, that is the sort of life that always brings satisfaction and happiness."

I stopped at Cooper's mail box, but Jimmy didn't budge. Didn't he remember that I was on my way to Charlotte? We were three miles from his house.

"Well, Libby Lou must be an exceptional girl. I didn't meet any one like her in Charlotte," I sighed.

"You would not meet girls like her in the places where you must have been," he said, still not beginning to get out. Instead he reached over and deliberately turned off the switch!

"Oh, don't you think so? Well, I'll have you know Abby is as good as most people are. I met a splendid young woman there, a high school teacher. And the young lawyer is as fine a young man as I want to know. They didn't drink and smoke a lot as some of the others did. Dorothea was as charming as Libby Lou. Of course, Libby Lou would be charming dressed in an evening gown and animated by excitement. She is a good mixer. She would be a divine dancer, for she is so light and quick," I said.

I didn't care a bit what I did to Jimmy. I was all out of harmony with him. I felt like giving him a push and driving on furiously.

He shook his head. "I can't imagine her in that sort of life, just as I have a hard time imagining you satisfied with it after the newness and glitter wear off. Libby Lou is pretty, but she is not physically beautiful. There is a light from within that adds beauty to her. Now, you are a good deal more attractive naturally than she is. You are charming, because you are full of life and pep. You have talent and ability. You would be a marvelous Christian and a wonderful influence for all that is right and good, for you would go all the way with the Lord. You would not compromise. You are having a hard time compromising with the devil. I know you pretty well, Betsann, and I know that you do not approve of all that you wish you could approve of. You recognize the worthlessness of life as you have seen it in Charlotte, the social life, the life of constantly hunting for a pleasure that will be more alluring than the one before. It would not satisfy you long."

"Thanks, just as if you meant it," I said, reaching for the switch.

Jimmy grabbed my hand and held it tight.

"Wait just one more minute, please. I do mean it, Bets. I mean it with all my heart. I am going to move into the old Miller place soon. I want you to help plan the remodeling of it, as we have talked about a lot of times. I may not stay in it long, for I am really expecting the Lord to come soon, just as Libby Lou was saying that Sunday. But I know He doesn't want us to sit still with folded hands to await His coming. Oh, Betsann, Beloved, I want you to be ready for Him when He comes!" Jimmy exclaimed, as he let go my hand and took my face between his two hands and kissed me hard!

I simply was too amazed to breathe!

Then he opened the door and was out before I had fully recovered.

"Goodbye, Betsann! I'll probably be in Asheville when you get back, but there won't be a day that I'll not be praying for you. Have a good time. God bless you and take care of you," he said, reaching out his hand.

I ignored the hand.

"Goodbye," I said, simply, managing to turn on the switch and step on the starter.

The old roadster went off with a jump that nearly upset me. I finally got it righted and was out of sight in no time. I was weeping as hard as I could and could hardly see to drive at all. I don't know what in the world ailed me. I wanted to scream and cry out loud! Finally I simply had to stop and get my handkerchief out and cry a minute before I could see to go on. I had a good notion to turn around and mail the ten dollars in. But that would never do! I couldn't let Jimmy Casper get the best of me like that. Not when he was going to Asheville to his own wedding! He might at least have told me about it instead of preaching to me the way he did, making me feel as if I were the greatest sinner in the whole world and was utterly and forever lost without any hope of redemption.

And to think he would mention the Miller place to me!

For years I have loved that old place. It is so picturesque, with the creek running right through it and the rocks and hills back of it, and the old, old flowers and trees and, oh, just everything! Jimmy and I had planned how we could make it into a perfectly gorgeous place for community gatherings, by enlarging the living room. It had such enormous old fireplaces in it, one in the cook room and another in the living room. Oh, we had never said we'd fix it up when we were married to each other, but we had planned and talked, and laughed a lot about it. And now Libby Lou was to live in *our* house!

Well, let them! I was going to live in Charlotte. I'd stay in my own apartment until Terry had a place ready for me. Then I'd invite Jimmy and Libby Lou to visit us and I'd show them a thing or two!

I stepped on the gas and made the little old roadster make up for lost time.

What was wrong with me? One minute I'd be wanting to laugh at the whole world and all its troubles. I'd be as happy and as gay as the birds that were flitting in the woods around me. Then the next thing I knew I'd be ready to bawl like a baby. One minute I wanted to stay a long time in Charlotte. The next I didn't want to go at all. One minute I didn't care if I was a sinner, just as Jimmy and all the rest thought I was. The next, I felt so condemned that I almost stopped the car so that I could stay still and pray until I was saved. I dared not pray, though, for I knew if I did I'd simply give up everything and surrender wholly to the Lord and that would be the end of my career. I was in a dreadful fix, as you can see.

I slowed up a little so that I could have more time to think. I was nearing Charlotte and I was still in a good deal of a muddle. Should I telephone Terry as soon as I reached town as he had suggested that I do? I became a little more courageous as I thought of him. He had been so perfectly grand in his letters. I recalled first one and then another of his epistles to me. They gave me fresh strength. The idea! I certainly was a silly to let Jimmy Casper upset all my plans, all my ambitions as he had done. Didn't I have any will of my own, any mind at all! Of course, I was going to Charlotte. Of course, I was going to stay until the very last minute on Tuesday. Of course, I'd telephone Terry the very first thing as soon as I reached a public telephone!

That settled, I stepped on the gas and with a lighter heart than I had had since I left home, I headed straight for the downtown district.

But I also headed smash, jam, slam into a car that stopped suddenly ahead of me!

It was my first wreck! I was scared stiff. The man in the other car was as mad as a hornet, but so was I!

"It wasn't my fault at all," I stormed at him, almost hysterically, for I had bumped my head till it ached. "You stopped suddenly without putting out your hand. How did I know you were going to stop?"

"You should have been watching!" he stormed back at me.

Of course, a motorcycle cop came up and we stopped quarreling. I explained and so did the man. The cop asked for our driver's licenses. Praise be! I had mine. The man had left his in his other coat pocket! That put things in my favor. The cop said the man was to blame and the man promised to pay for whatever damage he had done to my car. I couldn't find much damage besides a flat tire. The cop drove to a nearby filling station and the man gave me five dollars and we were all free to go on our ways. I don't know what the cop and the man decided. But I still was all a-flutter when my tire was fixed and I was ready to start again.

Right then and there, as I drove slowly and carefully on into town, I decided to go directly to the store, make that payment of ten dollars, turn squarely around, and go straight home. If Terry wanted to see me, he could come to my home and see me. I didn't live in Greenland! I was only about fifty miles from Charlotte. If he didn't care that much for me, well, if he didn't—

well, he could stay in Charlotte! I'd not even telephone Abby.

Elizabeth Ann, better known as Betsann, would go home!

CHAPTER VIII

SINCE it was Saturday, Charlotte seemed more crowded than ever. I couldn't find a parking place at all and kept feeling as if I were going to bump into someone every minute. After this I certainly would mail in my payments! Finally I paid fifteen cents and parked securely. Then I walked to the store. I had done no telephoning.

I still was a little nervous, and since it was nearly noon, I was hungry. But I entered bravely. Surely enough, Rust seemed to be watching for me. He was standing so that he faced the door. The man to whom he was talking had his back to the door. Rust beamed with smiles and left the man abruptly.

"Betsann!" cried Rust. Oh, not out real loud so as to attract attention, but so that I'd know how surprised and glad he was. "What a treat to set my eyes on you!"

He shook my hands in a most friendly fashion, and led me to where he had left the man.

"Look who is here!" he said to the man.

He turned.

"Terry!" I exclaimed.

"Betsann!" he exclaimed at the same time, snatching my hand and leaving it nearly helpless.

"Why didn't you let me know you were coming?" asked Terry.

"I did not know it in time myself," I admitted truthfully. "But it did not seem necessary."

"No, I just came in to get some office supplies and stood gossiping with Rust, and here you are! It's too good to be true!" he said, standing very close to me.

It was such a relief to see him, such a relief to be safely inside the store, that I wanted to cry. You may be very sure that I didn't however.

"How long are you staying this time, Bets?" asked Rust.

"Just until Tuesday," I said. You see, I changed my mind suddenly.

"Is that all!" Terry asked, looking keenly disappointed. "Well, we haven't a minute to lose then."

"I brought you ten dollars," I said to Rust, wanting to get through with business, and to get time to collect my scattering thoughts.

"Grand! You must have sold another story," he said, accepting the hard-earned ten.

"No," I laughingly replied, and I almost said I had picked cotton for it. "I wish I had!"

While Rust was making out his sales slip, Terry drew me to one side. "Have you had luncheon yet?" he asked, tenderly.

"No, not yet. I just got here," I told him.

"Wait till I phone my office and we'll go eat," he said, leaving me. "Want to use your 'phone," he nodded to Rust.

"Will you be at Abby's while you are here?" Rust wanted to know.

"Yes. She doesn't know I'm here yet, but of course, that's where I shall be."

"I'll be seeing you this evening then, around eight. Don't forget!"

I didn't actually know whether I wanted to see him or not, for I had hoped to have every minute I could with Terry. I wanted to be sure of him this time, but I couldn't be rude to Rust, for he had been rather nice to me. In fact, I remembered that he had even sort of said he loved me.

"That will be fun. Do come!" I urged him.

Terry reappeared.

"Business finished?" he asked.

I nodded.

"See you later, Rust. We are going out to eat. Too bad it's not your hour yet!" he said to Rust, laughing as he started out with me quite possessively.

"How did you come, Betsann? On the bus?" asked Terry, as we stepped outside.

"Oh, I drove!" I said, feeling dreadfully proud of the fact.

"Not all by yourself?" he asked, astonished.

"Why, certainly! It's only about fifty miles. I had a wreck as I came into town, though," I added, suddenly realizing that my head still felt bumped.

"A wreck?" gasped Terry. "Were you injured? Was your car damaged? Where is it now?"

"I bumped my head pretty hard," I said, lifting my hat a bit and wondering if the bump still showed. I could feel it with my fingers.

"You poor baby! Are you sure you aren't hurt anywhere else?" he asked, pity all over his face.

Poor baby indeed! I was no baby. I am my parents' oldest child!

"Oh, yes, I am quite sure. I simply bumped into a car because the driver stopped suddenly without giving any signal. No harm was done to the car except to give it a flat tire. The cop came and since the man didn't have his driver's license and I did have mine, I got out of it pretty easily and the man paid me five dollars damage," I explained, trying to show Terry that I was entirely capable of taking care of myself. "The car is parked down the street in a parking lot."

"Did you get the number of the car? Or the man's name? I'll take up the case for you and see that you receive something for this bump on your head. Why, you poor child, your nerves must have been all upset. Think what it has done to your nervous system. I can make quite a case out of it for you," Terry said, very professionally.

"Why, Terry, the man already paid me more than it cost to have the tire fixed. I even got a new inner tube out of it. And I really am not hurt. Of course, I didn't get his name or his number!"

"Listen here, Betsann, if ever you have another

wreck, no matter whether it is your fault or not, get the driver's name and the number of the car and tell him that your lawyer will handle the case. Then get in touch with me immediately. Understand? I don't want you getting hurt and not getting properly paid for it!" he declared.

"Oh, yes, I understand. And thanks heaps," I replied.

"Now, let's eat! How would you like to go where the salt of the earth have their luncheons?"

The salt of the earth! Must be some folks who were really important.

"I should like that very much indeed," I replied.

"Then we'll walk around here to the Superba Cafeteria. There the business girls and women and professional men eat. These people who make up the largest percentage of the city's elect wage earners I call the salt of the earth. They are neither the upper crust in society nor the more ordinary working class. They are the best the city has to offer," bragged Terry. "You have seen society at its gayest. Now see this greater army satisfy its hunger. And the food is good, too."

Thanks be to Abby, I had been in that very same cafeteria! I was so glad, for that was the first time I had ever been in a cafeteria and I certainly would have been dumb if Abby hadn't given me some lessons in choosing a tray of food from the quantities that were displayed.

Since I was hungry, I selected a filling meal. When we were seated at our table and my tray was placed before me, I glanced at Terry's.

"Is that all you eat?" I stammered, feeling perfectly ashamed of my own tray of substantial food.

"I seldom eat much at noon. Now I do eat a hearty dinner," he said, removing his lettuce, rolls, and coffee. "I am glad that you didn't have your appetite bumped out of you, though."

Oh, my appetite wasn't injured at all! It wasn't every day that I had the opportunity of selecting foods that I enjoy from so many kinds!

"But I feel selfish or something, sitting here devouring all this food while you nibble along like a bird," I confessed. "Won't you have some of mine?"

He laughed. "Betsann, you are undoubtedly the most refreshing child I have ever met. No wonder I love you. Go ahead and eat all you want, and if that isn't enough, we'll get some more. I wish I did have an appetite that demanded food, but sitting in an office is entirely different from living in the country where most of the time is spent out-of-doors. You are the very picture of health. Now take a good look at these girls around you. Oh, they are healthy enough, but they lack the freshness, the vigor that simply emanates from you."

I took a good look while I ate. I didn't want to keep him too long; so I tried to eat as quickly as I could without actually eating too fast. Well, I saw some very smart looking young ladies, I thought. Their clothes were good. Their manners seemed irreproachable to me. Except their smoking! I didn't try to count the girls and women that I saw smoking there in that public cafeteria. I had seen them when I was there with

Abby, but it was not noon then and there had been fewer in the room. Now it was full, and most of them were smoking. Even when one sat alone, she smoked.

"Terry, why do they smoke?" I asked.

He smiled. "Little girl, they enjoy it, I guess. Why do men smoke? Because we think we enjoy it. I shouldn't think you'd mind seeing a girl smoke a cigarette any more than you mind seeing people dip snuff back in your hills. Why, even some of my clients here in town take a dip of snuff when they think they can get by with it. I've even had some of my women ask me for a chew of tobacco. Now, I'd much rather see a woman smoke a cigarette than to soil her mouth with snuff or tobacco. Wouldn't you?" he asked, so suddenly that I was unprepared with an answer.

"I really had never thought much about it that way," I admitted. "I am so used to seeing women dip snuff and even chew tobacco. There is one old woman up home who smokes a pipe. Mom says she can remember when a good many women smoked pipes. But Mom never used any form of tobacco. Even Dad doesn't. Of course, I don't. To me it is all repulsive, for it is a nasty habit. I hate to see a girl spoil the shape of her mouth with snuff. I hate to see a man with tobacco juice staining his teeth and lips. I hate to smell stale tobacco on any one's breath. And I hate to see yellow fingers on a girl's hand. To me it is a common, expensive, filthy habit, whether it be man or woman, girl or boy, and in my mind a girl loses some of her womanliness when she smokes or uses tobacco in any form. There! That certainly is a long speech. Forgive me for seeming prudish, but I am also honest and that is my candid opinion on the tobacco question!" I concluded, trying to change to a more flippant tone.

Terry seemed to want to keep me ranting. "Well, I think a girl has as much right to smoke as a man has. It is up to her. I have seen some girls who smoked quite gracefully, and if they use cigarette holders, their fingers escape being stained. They simply have progressed from the snuff stage to the cigarette stage. It is another improvement our younger generation has made," he declared.

Well, I was rather surprised. I thought he was different that night at Abby's.

He looked at me sharply. "No, I think not. You are not that type. A cigarette would not be very becoming to you," he replied, slowly and thoughtfully.

What type was I? I was afraid to ask, for he had called me baby and child. He might have considered me too immature to try smoking. Maybe it would stunt my growth! Well, it was a relief that he didn't want me to smoke, for I would not have done it even to please him. There may not be a bit of harm in it, and it may be only because I am so back-woodsy and green that I don't like to see girls smoking. Lots of these girls were perfectly splendid looking.

By this time we had finished eating. He really had simply nibbled while I ate. I felt heaps better. My nerves were all steady again and I was glad that I was to stay over till Tuesday.

"Now what, little lady? Shall we go to a movie, or drive all over Charlotte, or swim, or what?" he asked, tucking my hand under his arm as we left the door.

"I really ought to go to Abby's," I said, remembering suddenly that she did not even know I was in town.

"Abby will keep. Let's take a long drive. My car is parked just around the corner. Then we'll come back and get yours and we'll go to Abby's. How's that?"

That suited me wonderfully. To have the whole afternoon with him! Sometimes I thought I loved him. Sometimes I thought I just naturally hated him. So I was going to have an opportunity of becoming a little better acquainted. His car was a sporty roadster, not shabby like Dad's poor old flivver. I felt very grand as I sat beside him, the breeze whizzing past us.

"This is a sight-seeing tour of the big city of Charlotte, or have you already seen all of Charlotte that you want to see?" he asked, as we headed away.

"I really know very little about Charlotte," I replied.

He was busy watching traffic and I was busy watching the people until we reached the residential section. Then we both had more time to talk. "When we get married, do you want a big house or one of these ducky little Spanish cottages?" he asked.

"Oh, let's have a ducky Spanish cottage," I replied lightly.

"Suits me. We'll have a big living room with a keen

floor and we'll dance when we want to right at home. Then I won't have to share you with any other man."

"Well! And I'll have a little room off in a corner where I can go and shut myself up and write. I'll have to do something while you are out defending the innocent and the guilty all day."

"Do you really write?" he asked, looking at me as if he didn't believe I knew much more than my A, B, C's.

"I am learning how. I have sold one story and I have another long one in a contest that is going to bring me five hundred dollars!" I informed him as impressively as I could.

"Who would have thought it? But then, I knew you were brilliant. What kind of stories do you write?"

"Oh, just any kind! That is why I like to come to Charlotte. It gives me such a wonderful opportunity to study life. When I really begin to sell more, I am going to move to Charlotte and have an apartment all of my very own."

"Grand! Then I can come to see you every night and you can read to me what you have written during the day and then when you think you love me enough, we'll get married. How's that?"

He seemed to take so much for granted!

"That may be perfectly fine," I admitted. Well, it might be!

"You have studied society as is, and you have seen the salt of the earth appease its hunger. Here is where society lives. The salt of the earth are scattered all over the city, here, in apartment houses, in the suburbs. My mother lives near here. How would you like to meet the family? Then we'll see some of the rest of this city."

I never even gave his family a thought. For some reason he seemed utterly disconnected to me. Of course, I was delighted to go to see his mother.

His house was rather pretentious. I felt a little trembly as I went up the broad steps. His mother was resting, but two of his sisters were in evidence. They wore lounging pajamas, and they were bare-footed. One, Norleen, did slip her feet into some sandals, but Hester, the older of the two (they were both older than I), paid not the slightest attention to her attire or lack of attire. There were magazines scattered about the room. On a table was a pitcher of iced-something with glasses that had been used. The room smelled of cigarettes. Presently his mother appeared. She was rather a large, florid woman, attired in a sleeveless, thin cotton frock that was quite becoming, if it had not been quite so juvenile.

The girls had not seemed any too gracious, but she was quite loquacious. She wanted to know all about the mountains and the farm and the family and everything one could possibly think of. A maid came in for the pitcher and glasses and returned with it refilled. I guess it was a grapejuice punch, but it was rather snappy. Must have had ginger ale in it. I drank mine and liked it, even if I did feel a little dubious as I did so. I remembered that Terry had been against liquor at Abby's that last night.

I was glad when we left. The girls are probably nice girls. I simply am not used to girls like them. And his mother, while not at all like my mother or even like Jimmy's mother, was all right, too. They are city folks. I'm a mountaineer. How like foreigners one or the other of us is!

I was thankful that Terry didn't ask me about his family as we drove away. He evidently thinks they are very smart and proper. It's just my ignorance.

We drove all over Charlotte. We went through the very poorest part there is, and through the cotton mill sections. I was very grateful, for Terry seemed to know conditions in each different place. I had a wonderful lesson in life that afternoon. Then we drove back down town.

"Betsann, let's not go to Abby's yet. Let's have dinner down here, then go some place to a movie, then dance till we are tired," suggested Terry.

I remembered Rust. And I was glad! I had been having a good time, but I was tired and for some reason I simply did not want to do all the things he had suggested. Already my mind was so full of things that I had to rest it a minute.

"Terry, I can never tell you how grateful I am to you for this marvelous afternoon, but I must go on to Abby's now. I am afraid she would not like it if I didn't go. And, oh, yes, Rust said he would be there at eight!" I added.

"Rust be hanged! You belong to me, not to Rust. Do you know that?" he asked, drawing me close to him.

"I am not exactly sure," I replied, truthfully.

"Sweet, you will be sure some day," he said, trying to kiss me!

I drew away from him and since we really were where someone could easily see us in the parking lot where my car was, he did not seek to demonstrate his affection any further. But I *knew* then that I was going to Abby's!

"If you won't stay all the evening with me, let's have dinner and then go to Abby's. We'll phone her and she can hold Rust till we get there. Will you do that for me, little lady?" Terry asked, humility itself.

"All right. And do you know how to reach Dorothea? I'd love to see her again. She could come and we'll have three couples then, if Joe is home," I consented.

Well, that is what we did.

"Have you ever eaten any Chinese food?" Terry asked.

"No, I haven't," I told him, wondering what would come next.

"Let's go to Loo Lin's and have a Chinese supper. You'll like it."

I was not so sure I'd like it, but because it was something new, we went.

The restaurant was upstairs. And every waiter was a Chinese! At first I felt dreadfully uncomfortable and a little frightened. I hope I didn't let Terry see how I felt. He seemed perfectly at home and did the ordering. Everything had a funny name, and I can't begin to tell what we ate, except rice and tea and candied ginger. It was right good.

"Terry, do you suppose these Chinamen are Christians?" I asked, when I didn't think any one could hear me.

"Christians?" repeated Terry, rather loudly, I thought. "What put that notion in your precious little head? I don't know. I'll ask the waiter."

"Oh, no!" I exclaimed. "He might not like being asked."

"If he doesn't like it, he'll never let you know that he doesn't. They have the most perfect control of their manners you ever saw."

Nevertheless I was trembling when the waiter came back with more tea. They never give one time to drink the tea before they bring some hotter, to take its place.

"Say, John, are you a Christian?" asked Terry, as the Chinaman set the teapot down.

John bowed. "Ah, yes, I am a Clistian. That's why my name is John! Once I believed in Buddha. Now I believe in Jesus!"

His face had the same sort of gleam that I have seen on Libby Lou's and on Jimmy's. It was a revelation to me.

"Do you go to church?" I asked, in rather a weak voice.

"Yes, mees. I work not on Sunday mornings. I go to worship." Again his face beamed.

As soon as he was gone, I asked Terry, "Are you a Christian?"

He laughed a little. "I guess I am. I went to Sunday School when I was a little fellow. I was baptized when I was an infant, and so I am a member of a church. I go now occasionally. My mother goes and she likes to have her offspring appear as decent as possible, so we all go sometimes to please her, to keep up appearances and to keep peace in the family, though sometimes it isn't very peaceable when the girls don't want to go."

"I just wondered," I murmured.

"Betsann, are you a Christian?" asked Terry, in mock seriousness.

"No, not yet," I replied.

That was the first time that I wanted to speak right up and say as that Chinaman had said, "Yes, I am a Christian!" Then I wanted to add, "But you are not!" I knew he wasn't. If that was the only reason he could give for being a Christian, I knew he simply was not one.

"Why, what makes you say that? If any one had asked me, I should have said that little Betsann was as perfect a little Christian as ever lived. You don't smoke. You don't drink. You don't seem wild about dancing. You even turned down a good picture for tonight. You won't let me kiss you. Why do you say you aren't a Christian, I'd like to know?"

I hung my head. I was ashamed to acknowledge it. "I have never accepted the Lord Jesus as my Saviour," I managed to say so that he could hear.

He looked queer when I glanced at him. "Great Scott, you are an innocent little dear. Sweet, don't you know all that is old-timey stuff? I guess you still have a mourners' bench back in your little church in the wilds. I guess the converts still really get religion. But we have outgrown a lot of that old stuff here in town. I guess all you have to do here is go up and shake hands with the preacher and tell him you want to join his church. If you've never been a church member before, you'll likely be sprinkled or baptized, whatever the church does, but that's about all there is to it. We don't have that emotional stuff now."

"We haven't outgrown the Lord up in the hills," I told him. And I was glad I said it!

"Oh, I didn't say we had outgrown the Lord. We just take a saner view of religion," he replied.

"You compromise with the devil!" I told him.

"Goodness! You'd make a good Christian, Betsann. I'll bet you wouldn't compromise with the old devil," he said, laughing, as he arose.

"No, I wouldn't," I declared.

"Now what?" he asked, when we were on the street.

"We promised Abby we would come to her house as soon as we ate. Let's keep our promise," I said.

"Do you always keep your promises?" he asked, as we started towards our parking places.

"I always try to. If I know I can't keep one, I don't make it," I assured him.

"See what a fine girl you are! Of all men, your husband will be the luckiest, and I expect to be the man. What do you say, little Betsann?" he asked, taking hold of my arm and drawing me very close to him.

"I don't know yet, Terry. I am not sure, and since I am not, I do not want to promise," I said, staying close to him to see if I should be any more certain.

But I wasn't. I have read stories about how thrilled people who are in love with each other are; and how the slightest touch makes their hearts thump like everything. But I wasn't thrilled and my heart behaved itself quite normally. I had a nice, comfortable, friendly sort of feeling, but I really was disappointed because that was all. I had come to Charlotte with eager, sweet, loving anticipations. At least I had left home with them and had kept them until I had met Jimmy. But the afternoon had held so much. Things had seemed so different. Terry was not quite the same as he had seemed on paper. I simply did not know, but I did not think I was really in love, not with Terry.

"I shan't urge you till you are sure, sweet. But remember, I'll keep on loving you," he said tenderly, as we reached the cars.

He trailed me as we went to Abby's. And as I drove I remembered that Jimmy had said, "I'll be praying for you every day!"

One man praying for me.

Another man loving me.

And which did I prefer?

Right that very minute I decided that I needed Jimmy's prayers more than I needed Terry's love!

Before I had a chance to retire that night, before Sunday in Charlotte had ceased to be Sunday, I was sure that I needed Jimmy's prayers most.

CHAPTER IX

I DROVE on into the extra garage and then I slipped in the back way while Terry waited for me on the front veranda. I simply did not want to risk being alone with him on the shadowy porch. That's a sign I didn't love him, isn't it?

Abby was in the kitchen. "Abby, run and bring Terry in from the front. I've slipped in this back way," I exclaimed, as I rushed into the house.

Abby called Joe and the next I heard he was ushering in Terry with much ado while Abby was going upstairs with me. Rust and Dorothea were already there. I knew Terry and Joe and the other two would have a good time, while I made myself look a little more presentable, with Abby's efficient help. After a quick shower, I slipped into the yellow organdy. I felt heaps better, too, when we were ready to go down to the company.

At first I thought Terry looked a little peeved, but he soon recovered. For a while we had a good time just talking. They wanted to know all about what I had been doing. I didn't think cotton picking would

122

thrill them much, so I told them about Marjorie's party and then we played some of the games that Libby Lou had taught us that night. We had a lot of fun. They all seemed to enjoy them as much as they did dancing or anything I had seen them do. The radio wasn't even turned on. We laughed till our sides ached, just as we had done at Marjorie's party. Rust declared that he hadn't laughed so heartily in a long time. Terry had to wipe his eyes more than once. Then Abby served us some ice cream and cake that she had prepared after she had known we were coming! That's what one can do with an electric refrigerator. It's a lot different out in the hills.

As we talked, we drifted into a more serious sort of conversation. I think Dorothea started it.

"Suppose you go to Sunday School with me in the morning, then, Betsann," Dorothea said, after we had been discussing our churches and Terry had aired his views as he had done to me. "As far as I know now, I shan't have to teach a class. I am a substitute teacher for the Young People's Department. I don't often have to teach. I belong to a grand class of young business women and we have a wonderfully good teacher. If you care to go, I'll come for you."

"I'd be delighted," I assured her. Then I almost bit my tongue. Suppose the wonderfully good teacher should make me feel like a dreadful sinner again! I had been so busy since landing in Charlotte that I had succeeded in putting away the things that Jimmy and

Libby Lou had said, to a great extent. But I'd stick by my word.

"Haven't you outgrown Sunday School yet, Dorothea?" asked Rust.

"Why, no, certainly I haven't. Have you?" she asked.

"Long ago! I used to be compelled to go to Sunday School whether I wanted to go or not. My mother was a very religious sort of person. Oh, I don't mean that she carried much of it home and went around talking and singing and praying all the time, but she did attend church regularly. She saw to it that her young hopefuls always attended Sunday School and then sat miserably beside her in the church services where we never did understand much that the preacher was saying. Sometimes he told stories about David and the giants and bears and such, but we never believed them.

"During the week our mother was like all other mothers. She was gay and full of life. She danced and went to the theaters and took us sometimes. But on Saturday nights we had to prepare our Sunday School lessons. When company came, Father always had us bow our heads and he asked a blessing upon what we had to eat, unless the company was more religious than he was. Then he turned the job over to the company. Well, I made up my young mind, what I had, that I'd quit going to Sunday School just as soon as I was my own man. And I did.

"Now when I hear of an extra good preacher in town, or some folks in the store rave about some evangelist who is here, I go occasionally. I don't belong to any particular church, and so I go where I please, be it Christian Science or Unitarian or what not. I like the music in some churches, so when I'm feeling down and out I go where the music is good. That's my brand of religion," Rust concluded, flicking the ashes from his fourth cigarette.

"Don't you think about the time when you are going to die?" I asked for I had thought about it a lot lately.

"Why, no! There's plenty of time for that. I'm still rather young and am the healthiest of my mother's six. I'm thinking of living just now. Anyway, I am not so sure that there is much after death. I think we had better make the most of the life we have right now. It's the only one we are sure of. And we aren't sure of its lasting very long, with all the accidents there are these days, and so many sudden deaths. This life is pretty good. I'd like to live a hundred years and watch the changes, if they come as fast as they have within the last few years. Then I'd be willing to go back to dust and that would be the end. Is any one sure of a life beyond the grave?" he asked all of us, glancing all about the room.

"Yes," replied Dorothea without hesitating. "All who believe the Bible are sure of life beyond the grave. It is true some believe only the part they want to accept and omit the other, but that is not right. If one accepts one part of the Bible as God's infallible Word, he must accept it all. All of us like to believe in God's heaven as being a most wonderful place that He has prepared for all who believe in Him. But there are not as many who like to accept hell as being as much of a fact as heaven. No one ever likes to consider discomfort, whether it is here now or expected. Consequently we like to think of the ease and delight of heaven, but we spurn any sort of teaching about torment or a place for the unbelievers. A good many people will some day awake from the dead and find themselves just where they thought no one ever would go. I don't want to be among them myself," she concluded.

"There's not much danger, Dot," said Terry, laughingly. "You are about as good a girl as Betsann is. She's the best I ever saw!"

They all laughed, but it seemed rather a forced laugh. I felt myself turn desperately red, for that wasn't what Jimmy thought being a Christian was at all. I wished I could tell them, but I simply didn't know how. Dorothea took it up.

"I am not good," she declared, positively. "I wish I were. No one knows the dreadful times I have. In the first place, I am sure I am far too worldly to merit any sort of a reward, as the Bible teaches those who deserve it will receive. I dance, because I like to dance. It does me no harm. I love the motion, the rhythm, the exercise. I don't stop to consider what my influence may mean to any other person. I don't consider that from the dance has originated every sort of vice. Some one asked me once if I would ask the Lord to be a partner in a dance. Well, I'd certainly not ask Him to accompany me to some dances that I have attended, for too many of the dancers drank till they were tipsy and everything was downright wicked. But if I could invite Him to dance where every one was decent, where every one danced simply for the pleasure there was in the dance itself, I believe it would be different.

"It's the same with cards. I thoroughly enjoy a keen game. I like to have to fight to win. And I often win. But, I know that there is more gambling done with cards than with any other device. Every game that is played with prizes is a way to gamble. Yet I play. The thing I enjoy is the means of breaking whole families.

"I enjoy a good movie. I don't care about a lot of pictures that I have seen, but I have seen pictures that were educational and entertaining. I never stop to consider the private lives of the actors and the actresses. Too many are deplorable. On the other hand, neither do I stop to consider if a merchant is the right sort of man. If he has what I want, I buy it, no matter what he is personally. So what's the difference? I don't drink, but it isn't because I am too religious to drink. I don't like the taste of any sort of liquor that ever I have tried. Anyway, I constantly see too much of what drink does to the human being. We've heard a lot of talk about personal liberty and personal rights. The man who wanted to drink fought prohibition because it took away from him his personal liberty. Yet the same men will drink till they are not themselves at all. Gone is their liberty. Gone is everything decent and respectable and responsible in their lives. I conclude, therefore, that drink would do the same for me, so I leave it alone.

"It is about the same with cigarettes. I've tried smoking, but I don't like it. I don't like the taste that lingers in my mouth after a cigarette. I wouldn't have my fingers stained for a million cigarettes. And besides, I have read and studied till I know the physical harm that tobacco can do, especially to a woman. Some day I might marry. If I do, I want children. If my children should die or be physically weak or mentally deficient because their mother was saturated with nicotine, I'd simply never forgive myself.

"Since I am started, I might as well go the rest of the way. We are all pretty well acquainted, so I know no one will misunderstand what I am about to say. I have guarded my purity of body simply because for me to have done otherwise would have been positively repulsive. I have never been able to understand how any girl could let any boy or man touch her in any but a decent, respectful way. When I marry, I want my husband to be the first man to have had any sort of privileges that only a husband should have. Then marriage will mean more to me than it can possibly mean to a girl to whom things that are sacred to marriage have become common.

"There! I do not claim to be good! I am not. I believe in the Lord Jesus as my Saviour. I wish I were fully and completely surrendered to Him. I am not. I don't know why. As I say, I thoroughly enjoy too much that is considered worldly. Yet, if I were the sort of

Christian that I should be, I should be glad to give it all up to Him. And according to my Bible, He would so completely fill my life that I'd not miss the things I give up. Some day, I hope I shall reach the place where I shall be willing to make a complete surrender," she concluded softly.

"Dorothea, and everybody else," began Terry, just as I was going to tell them about Libby Lou and how completely surrendered she is, "let me ask you all something. Before the World War, didn't everybody look at things a little more narrowly than we do now? Then after the War when the whole world was upside-down and no one knew what he wanted, didn't we all go sort of mad? Young people were trying everything, much to their own disgust, much to their delight, and finding out that some things were not worth the effort.

"Now we are trying to find a landing place, a stopping place. Some of the things that we all frowned upon, we have begun to accept. Look at women's dress, for instance. The first short dresses were perfectly shocking. Now if a woman should wear a long dress on the street, people would turn around and gaze at her. Women have learned some sense about clothes. We aren't all ready to admire girls who trot around in trousers, yet, and we who live in inland towns, still look upon the bathing suits as not quite enough covering. Yet when I was at the coast, no one seemed to pay any attention to them.

"It's the same with dancing, card playing, drinking, and all the old vices. We've seen so much, tried so much, that what we used to consider sin, we think very little about. When we fully recover ourselves, we shall discover that we have an entirely different standard from what we once had. Religion is taking a different attitude about a good many things. Some churches give dances for their young people. A good many have picture shows even on Sunday nights. If you watch the Society notes, you'll find that the best church members attend numerous card parties, dinner dances, and what not. We simply have broadened. It remains to be seen whether this world will be better or worse for the new ideals we have. At any rate, there are so many different forms of religion now that if one isn't comfortable in one church, he can soon find one that is more to his liking," he finished—rather lamely, I thought.

"I think you are about right," chimed in Joe. "We all have to do some standard setting for ourselves. I think if we decide what we want out of life and go after it, we have about all we can do. Now I want a comfortable living, but I don't crave many luxuries. I don't expect always to be light-hearted, and happy. The sun doesn't always shine. If it did, we'd get rather tired of the monotony. We need a few hardships to make us appreciate the soft snaps that come our way. I want to become a more competent worker every year. I don't want to slump, but I want to keep up with the times in my line of business. This takes nerve, for it is often easy to drift and not advance with the few who do advance. Well, I want to cultivate that variety of nerve. Yet, I want to have fun, to be able to enjoy pleasures, to be able to enjoy beauty in things around me, my wife included.

"I don't have any ambition to cheat, to get ahead of any one simply to be ahead. When it comes time to die, I don't want to be head-over-heels in debt; so I'll try to live within my income and still put away a little for the knocks that come to everyone. I want to be able to face any man and have him call me friend instead of enemy. That's my creed.

"As far as God and the church are concerned, I think one form of religion is about as good as another. Of course, I believe there was a Creator. I'm not an evolutionist, for I think too much of myself to believe that I sprang from any lower form of animal life. I believe there is a God now who takes care of the universe. I don't know much about this personal stuff. To me, He is too big and busy to be bothered about individuals. Imagine the President of the United States being a listener to every little personal desire and want of his subjects! So what happens to me after death, I am willing to leave to the great God. In the meantime, I'll get all out of this life that I can, making the most of each day and its opportunities."

"I disagree with you both in some things," Dorothea was brave enough to say. "In the first place, I believe that God is a personal God. He is not limited as the President or any other human being is limited. I am sure I do not know how He does it, but I do believe that He knows about us each individually. That is why I am often ashamed because I do not serve Him more whole-heartedly. I believe the Bible, and the Bible certainly teaches that He knows each one, and has from the foundation of the world. I don't understand it all, but it is a comfort to me to believe it and I certainly have nothing to lose if I am not right and much to gain if I am.

"I believe in prayer. Even I, worldly and often sinful as I am, have had too many prayers answered and too definitely not to believe that God hears and answers prayers. And I do not believe that one religion is as good as another. There is no other way under heaven whereby man can be saved except through faith in the Lord Jesus, who is God's only Son. All religions that leave Him out, all religions that deny His deity, His death, His resurrection, are as nothing. One might as well worship the old Roman gods or a heathen idol as to worship a religion that is stripped of its saving power. I know there are all sorts of churches springing up and all sorts of merging of churches, but as long as the world lasts there will be the New Testament church for those who will accept the true religion of Christ. I believe that I belong to that kind of a church.

"Suppose you all come to church in the morning. Dr. Beebe is a good preacher. You will enjoy his sermon even if you are not able to agree with everything he says. At least, he will give you something to think about. I'll call for Betsann for Sunday School. I'd be glad to have all of you come for that service, but since most of you have declared for yourselves a vacation from Sunday School, I shan't insist. You are missing a lot, though, I will say. Then all of you come to church and let's go some place for dinner. How about the whole bunch of you coming home with me for dinner? Mother will be delighted and I'll get on the good side of Delia. We'll have a grand time."

Well, there was first one excuse and then another, but none would hold water, as my Dad says. Finally it was so decided. Then since it was late, really nearly one on Sunday morning, we separated for the night. Dot was to call for me at nine-thirty!

I never had felt so keyed up. I never had been through so many different experiences in one day. I tossed and rolled. I wanted more than anything to get out of that bed and get down on my knees and beg the Lord to forgive all my sins and save me. But then a little, hard voice would seem to whisper to me, "Silly, it's just because you are so tired and your poor head is so full of new ideas and thoughts. Go to sleep. There's still plenty of time. Don't create a fuss here. You might shout like some of the good sisters out in the hills. What would Abby and Joe think? Why, they would think that you had simply lost your mind, of course!

Finally I slept. Oh, I wish I had prayed, if it had taken me the rest of the night to be saved! Why, why, oh, why was I so hard-headed, so hard-hearted?

CHAPTER X

OH, what a Sunday! By bedtime was there ever a girl who was as utterly miserable, sick, and wretched as I? I certainly hope not. I hope there never will be. I didn't want to live and I certainly did not want to die!

I was ready when Dorothea came for me. We went to the largest church that I had ever attended. Her class had a room all by itself, a lovely room with the daintiest sort of curtains and pictures on the wall and a piano and a table and chairs and books and flowers. It made me want to stay in it a long time. Dorothea introduced me to a number of the girls and older girls. They were all as friendly as could be and they had a most enjoyable time as they waited for the lesson hour. Presently the teacher came, and I fell in love with her immediately. She was neither young nor old, but she was very attractive, very much alive, and very fond of her girls, as she called them all. There were the usual preliminaries, I guess, before the lesson period. This was the first time I had been in a Sunday School class like this. At first it seemed more like some sort of club, for there were committee reports, secretary reports, records to take and keep, and various things. But after prayer by one of the girls, the teacher was asked to take charge.

The lesson was from the eleventh chapter of John. As soon as Mrs. Simpson stepped forward, there was an expectancy, a hush, an eagerness that permeated the room. The whole chapter had previously been read aloud by a girl. Now they waited for the lesson.

"What will you think if I center our lesson on only one verse?" asked Mrs. Simpson. "That is what I am going to do. Now each of you look again at the chapter and in just a moment, let me see if anyone has chosen the verse that I have chosen."

You may be very sure every one of us was looking at our Bibles or Testaments. I had a Bible that belonged to the class. They kept a supply on hand for just such as I. I skimmed through as fast as I could, thinking it would be the twenty-third, then the thirty-fifth or thirty-sixth. I had not read the entire chapter before Mrs. Simpson said, "Time!"

There were several different verses that were chosen, but some did select the right one, the twenty-eighth.

"At the close of this verse there is a statement. I want to read this to you from five different translations. First the King James, which most of you have, 'The Master is come and calleth for thee.' Next, the Montgomery, 'The Teacher is here and is asking for thee.' Third, from Goodspeed, 'Here is the Master, asking for thee.' The fourth is from Weymouth, 'The Rabbi is here and is asking for thee,' And fifth, I find in the Moffatt translation, 'The Leader is here and He is calling for you.' These translations have been very interesting to me. I thought they would be to you. Of course, the one point is the same in all. The Lord Jesus had come and He was asking for Mary. Martha had gone out to meet Him, but Mary had sat still. I shan't say perfectly still, for I suspect she wanted to go out to meet Him, too, but she must have known down deep in her heart that He would come for her or send for her. Perhaps she felt that someone had to stay with all the Jewish friends who were there in the house, mourning with the sisters.

"Then the word came, blessed word from her blessed Lord and Master. 'He is here, Mary! He has come at last. And He is asking for you!' I am sure it did not take Mary many seconds to excuse herself and go out to meet the Lord. Many of the friends followed her. At first they did not know exactly why she left so hurriedly, but they soon found out. She led those who followed her to the Saviour."

Mrs. Simpson kept on with the picture of it all so that I could see every bit of it. I had never listened to so graphic a picture and discussion of a Bible scene and passage. I felt as if I were right there with them all. I wish I could remember all that she said, but I can't.

When she led us to the tomb and we had seen the Master weep and had felt the thrill of triumph in our own hearts when Lazarus arose from the dead, Mrs.

Simpson stepped a little nearer to the girls and with the tenderest voice I ever heard, she said, "Girls, the Master is come and calleth for thee! If you are a Christian, He is calling to you to follow Him more closely. It had seemed impossible to those who stood there for Him to bring back Lazarus from the dead. Even the sisters had said, 'I know he will rise again at the resurrection at the last day. But not now, Lord! Don't ask me to believe that he will come forth from that grave. Why, he has been dead so long that he smells foul.' Have you a Lazarus? Is he so buried in your inner life that you think nothing can dislodge him? Jesus can!

"Oh, girls who are Christians, Jesus wants to prove to you how much He loves you. He loved you enough to die for you so that you might have the salvation that He has already bestowed upon you. He loves you yet more. He has many other blessings that he would pour out upon your lives if you will but accept them. Open every wee corner of your heart and let Him come in. Let Him in the form of the Holy Spirit cleanse you from every secret sin, from every habit that would separate you the least bit from the full joy of your salvation. Give to Him the burdens that you try to bear. Let Him be your all in all.

"And girls who are not yet saved, He is calling you!" she said, almost in a whisper. I felt as if she had said, "Elizabeth Ann Ellison, He is calling you!" My heart jumped. Oh, I wanted to jump up and tell all those girls that I heard Him and was ready to answer Him. But I didn't! That same little hard, sneering voice down inside of me said, "Silly! Sit still. Don't make a scene here in this dignified classroom!" Well, I sat still, but I was perfectly miserable. I tried not to listen, but I heard her anyway. The minutes seemed like hours. Then she quoted these lines, that I got later from Dot:

> *"I heard Him call, 'Come, follow Me!'*
> *My gold grew dim.*
> *My soul went after Him.*
> *I rose and followed. That was all.*
> *Who would not follow if she heard Him call?*
>
> *"And when He comes and calls thee*
> *Arise and follow fast.*
> *His way may lead through the darkness,*
> *But it leads to the Light at last."*

"Dear girls, the Master has come. He came to Mary in that manger so long ago. The Master is come. He is here this very minute. He is speaking to every heart here, calling some into a deeper experience with Him, calling some to surrender definite known sins, calling some to accept Him as Saviour. And, girls, the same Jesus, the same Master will come again. Will you be ready? What will you do with Jesus today?"

Oh, if she would only hush! If she would only say we were dismissed! But she prayed and I felt as if I'd simply smother. I had a terrific time to keep from crying out, but finally she was through and we were dismissed. Somehow I managed to speak to those who spoke to me. Finally we were out in the air. Then I saw Abby and Joe and Terry and Rust. Slowly the spell was broken and I began to feel a little more like myself. How I wished we weren't going to have to hear a "good" sermon! But there would be so many people in the huge church that perhaps I would not feel as if the preacher meant me. We laughed and joked a bit before we went in. When we were finally seated in the great big auditorium that would have held ten times more people than were there, I felt fairly comfortable, especially when I could keep my mind off that lesson about John 11:28.

Well, the pipe organ was simply grand! I could have listened and listened. I had heard a pipe organ before over the radio at Abby's, but never, never had I actually been in one's presence. Wouldn't I love to be able to play one! Then the choir that wore those funny, ugly white gowns sang with the organ. I didn't catch many of the words of the songs. However, the music was wonderful and the sound of their blended voices was lots better than ours in the hills. Maybe the congregation is not supposed to understand all the words. It was different when they sang hymns and we all had books to look at.

Of course, the preacher had a lot of things to do that ours doesn't, but he finally got to his preaching.

"Beloved," he began, (Jimmy called me beloved once! Now wasn't I too silly to remember that at that moment when the preacher was calling his whole flock beloved!) "I want to tell you this morning what the

Lord Jesus says you are in His Word. You may not feel as if you merit all that He says you are. If you do not, He can help you to become all that He wants you to become. While I want to talk chiefly to Christians, I do so trusting that those who may not know the Lord Jesus yet as your own personal Saviour, may find something in His words that will make you want to become all that He is expecting you to be. There are seven things that my Lord and Master tells me that I am. There are seven things that your Lord and Master tells you that you are. Will you examine yourselves and see if He finds you living up to His expectations this morning?"

I got my pencil and a little piece of paper. I thought maybe Libby Lou might like to know what the Lord Jesus thought she was. And Jimmy.

The first reference he gave was Matthew 5:13, "Ye are the salt of the earth." He had an altogether different sort of meaning for that phrase than Terry had when he took me to the cafeteria where his salt of the earth dined. The Bible says only Christians are the salt of the earth, and I am sure not all those who were in that cafeteria were Christians. As the salt of the earth, the preacher said, Christians should have the characteristics of salt; that is, they should purify their surroundings, they should preserve the church and Christianity through their influence as God's followers, and they should retain their savor, even as salt does unless it becomes mixed with something else. So it is with Christians. They lose their savor when they get mixed up with the world.

In the same reference the Bible says, "Ye are the light of the world." Since Christians are the light of the world, they should be flashing rays of God's love to the uttermost parts of the earth, beginning from the place where each one lives, and that means in his very own home among his own people and kin, in the places where Christians work or study or stay most of the time.

Then the preacher turned to John 15:5. "I am the vine, ye are the branches." He reminded those city folks that a branch could not bear fruit unless it abides in the vine. The vine gives life to the branch. So unless Christians as branches abide in the Lord Jesus as the Vine, they will dry up and wither and become useless.

Next he went to the Old Testament and read from Isaiah 44:8, "Ye are even my witnesses." He quoted a chorus from a song:

> *"Reading you, yes, reading you,*
> *Knowing whatever you say or do,*
> *Morning and evening and night time, too*
> *Somebody surely is reading you."*

Then he asked, "So, beloved, what is the gospel according to you? Are you being God's witnesses? This is His only plan of winning a lost world. The message was first given to the disciples. They were His witnesses. Some one down through the ages has been faith-

ful, for here we are and we have been told the Good
News. Yet we are also told to go and tell still others.
Oh, how much we tell! Is it all to the glory of the
Lord? As others read you moment by moment do they
become more deeply in love with your master? I want
to be such a witness that I shall not be ashamed to
meet my Lord face to face some of these days. How
about you?"

I felt like hiding my face right that minute, you may
be sure.

Well, he went back to the New Testament for his
next "Ye are." He read John 15:14, "Ye are my friends."
Then he read the condition of friendship with the
Lord, "If ye do whatsoever I command you." All of
God's commands were given in love and for our own
good, therefore we should eagerly seek to know them
and to obey them. It is a privilege not lightly to be
considered, this possibility of being a friend of the
Lord God.

He read then from First Corinthians 3:16 and 17,
"Ye are the temple of God and the Spirit of God dwell-
eth in you." Then he preached about how we should
take care of our bodies because they are the temple of
God and the Holy Spirit is dwelling in the heart of all
believers. Even as we try to keep the churches and
places of worship in beautiful condition, we should
endeavor still more to keep this living temple in perfect
health, in perfect purity, in perfect cleanliness of habit,
deed, and thought.

What a lot real Christians have to think about! But

it certainly would mean something if one really lived
up to all that a Christian should live up to. It seems to
me that a half-way Christian is no Christian at all! So
much would be gained by going all the way with the
Saviour. I do want to be a Christian. For a long time
I have wanted to be, but I want to more than ever
now, for it is so worth while. I am beginning to see
things differently.

The final "Ye are" was found in Hosea 1:10, "Ye are
the sons of the living God." Then he added, "And if
children, then heirs of God, and joint heirs with Christ."
As children of God, the King of kings, we (I can't help
saying we. He said it, you see, and I am going to be
one of the we's soon!) we are princes and princesses!
Children of God, members of God's great family, loved
of Him, watched over by Him, pitied by Him like as
a father pitieth his children. I wondered what those
folks were thinking who say God doesn't consider the
individuals.

Well, the preacher finally began to close. "And it
doth not yet appear what we shall be, but we know
that when He shall appear, we shall be like Him. Beloved, don't you feel like shouting, 'Hallelujah! Praise
the Lord! Amen!'? Surely your hearts are shouting,
even though your lips are still. Let us pray!"

While the heads were all bowed and no one was
looking at me, I just had to weep a little. I had been
left out of all the seven things that God says Christians
are! I felt as if a door had been closed in my very face.
But I was determined that the door should not stay

closed. Just as soon as I got home, I was going to surrender myself to the Lord!

It did not take us long to start to Dorothea's home.
Rust went with her, I with Terry, and Joe and Abby
drove their car.

"How did you like that sermon, little lady?" asked
Terry.

I had so hoped no one would ask me! I wasn't ready
to tell anyone how I felt.

"I think it was a good sermon. Don't you?" I asked
him.

"Oh, yes, it was very good, I guess, for anyone who
likes that sort of preaching. But it is too impractical.
No one could live up to the standards he set this morning."

"I don't think it is impossible to live a surrendered,
consecrated life. I met a girl this summer who certainly
seemed to. She was about the gayest, happiest person
I ever saw, too. Of course, she was in love with a pretty
nice young man and that helped her to be happy, I
suppose, but she was what I'd call a real Christian,"
I replied.

Terry looked at me. He laughed. "Honey, you are
such a serious little lady sometimes. Don't let the things
you heard this morning get next to you and spoil your
day. If Dr. Beebe had lived forty years ago and had
preached that sermon, it might have seemed a little
more possible. But times have changed. People have
changed. We can't live the lives our devout parents
and grandparents lived. We haven't time!"

Ahead of us there was the scream of brakes, the crash of glass, and before either of us realized that anything was happening we, too, had slammed into the two wrecked cars. It was done so quickly that no one seemed to know how it had happened or just what had happened. The jolt threw me against the windshield and then back into the corner of the seat with such force that I simply passed out entirely. When I revived, Terry was pulling me from my corner and asking me if I were hurt. I stared at him and almost fainted again, for blood was all over his face.

"Betsann, listen to me. Don't faint again!" begged Terry.

"I'm all right," I managed to say.

"Are you, honey? Are you sure?" he kept asking, shaking me a little.

"Yes, I'm all right. Are you hurt?" I blurted, blinking to keep back the tears.

"I got a little cut, but I'm all okay. The cop doesn't want us to leave for a minute. Are you able to stay?"

I did feel better, and I saw so much going on around us that I forgot my bumps. I even forgot Terry's bleeding face.

"Is she dead?" I whispered to Terry, as I watched some men carry a woman from one of the wrecked cars.

"Maybe not. They can't tell. It is a bad smash-up. Are you all right?"

"Oh, yes, I just got bumped, I guess. Look, Terry, there's a little child! Terry, how many were hurt?" I gasped.

"One car had only two people in it and the other had four. The first two have been taken away in an ambulance. And there comes another one for these."

We didn't say a word then, for we couldn't. The woman and the child were placed in that ambulance and whizzed off as another came up for the man and a boy. Then a cop and a doctor came up to us. Evidently Terry had not tried to move the car, for it was still jammed against the big sedan that was smashed.

"See if you can move out now, Mr. Lane. Are you sure neither of you is much hurt?" asked the cop.

"We haven't investigated very thoroughly yet, but I think we aren't badly injured," Terry replied, smiling, though it was a rather feeble smile.

The car did not seem badly damaged. He succeeded in backing it from the wreck and then got out and examined it.

"Besides bent fenders, I think it's okay. If you don't want us any more, I'd better get this young lady to her friends," Terry told the men.

The doctor had been watching me, though I didn't know it. Every few seconds I'd feel dreadfully queer and swimmy-headed. I closed my eyes for a minute and I felt a hand on my arm.

"Swallow this, young lady," someone said.

I swallowed. It was a little pill and I wasn't much good at swallowing pills without water. However, I did it.

"If she isn't all right when you get home, you'd better take her to the office, Terry," the doctor said. "You'll be all right when you get that cut dressed. It's not deep."

Why, I was all right. I just bumped my head again and it made me feel woozy. I tried to be a little more pert as we drove on to Dot's. We were almost there when we hit the wrecked cars, and it didn't take many minutes to arrive.

As the car stopped before the house, the four of them ran to meet us. We didn't present a very beautiful sight with fenders bent, Terry's face still rather bloody and dirty, and me all shaky and white.

"What has happened?" they all asked at once.

I wanted to cry, cry out loud and long. I felt downright hysterical. Abby grabbed me on one side while Dot held the other arm. They didn't wait to hear all that Terry said. They took me straight to Dot's room, took off my hat and shoes and stretched me out on Dot's bed. By that time her mother was in the room.

"Suppose you leave her to me for a little while," I heard a sweet, quiet voice say. I didn't open my eyes till I felt a cool, firm hand on my forehead.

"Lie perfectly still, dear, and close your eyes. You aren't hurt, but you had a severe shock and you need to relax and be still a few minutes. Cry if you want to. Your nerves are still a little jittery, but you will feel as good as new in a little while," Dot's mother said, smiling at me and still rubbing something on my head.

I didn't want to cry so much then, for she seemed so quiet and cool and unexcited. I did close my eyes and relax to the soothing effect of her touch.

Presently I was able to begin to realize what had happened and what might have happened. I wasn't really severely injured. Neither was Terry. But others had been. Others perhaps had been hurled into eternity without a second to prepare for it, if they were not already prepared. I might have been one of them! Terry might have been! I shuddered.

"You feel better. Don't you, dear?" asked Mrs. Brooks gently.

I opened my eyes. When I did so, I was looking into the depths of the bluest, kindest eyes that I had seen since I had left my own mother's eyes. And her hair was white and soft, just like a halo about her face.

"Yes, I do feel better, thank you. But, Mrs. Brooks, I might have been killed!" I said.

"Yes, you might have been, but the dear Lord has spared your life for His own purpose. Thank Him and seek to know what that purpose is. If you are feeling well enough now, we shall go down to dinner. If you would rather, though, I shall have yours served here," she said, helping me to stand.

At first I was a little dizzy, but I soon felt all right. My head throbbed, but I could endure that. I did not want to spoil the afternoon.

The food was perfectly delicious, but I was thankful when they began to talk about more pleasant things than wrecks. We did have a most enjoyable visit, for Mrs. Brooks kept our minds occupied with the right sort of bright things.

Some one suggested driving, but that certainly did

not appeal to me! I dreaded having to go home with Abby and Joe, much less take a drive for pleasure. We just stayed with Dot until about five, when Joe and Abby said they had an engagement with some other friends. I went with them, thus leaving Terry and Dot and Rust.

Their engagement was to play bridge with those friends. What a way to close that Sunday!

CHAPTER XI

"YOU be careful how you play," Joe said to Abby, when we started to the Carters, "You had better not play for too much money, either. We lost so much the last time we played with them that we had better be a little more careful today."

"Suppose you watch your own step, big boy," Abby flared up, and I was surprised. I guess I am stupid, but I didn't see anything in what he had said to make her so angry. I thought it was pretty good advice. "If I remember correctly it was you who lost the most money."

"Oh, yeah? Well, it was you who did the rotten playing that made me lose," he muttered.

"Look here, Mister, if you don't want to go, say so, and we'll go to a movie or back home. I'm not so anxious to go and play with those dumb-bells till the wee small hours. I didn't make the plans. You did it," stormed Abby.

"Oh, well, drop it. We'll have to go for a while. If you don't like it, you can claim a headache and we'll leave. I didn't mean to start a row," Joe tried to pacify Abby.

My head was aching and I still felt none too well. I wished they would go home, but I could also see that they were both determined to go and both determined to play just to suit themselves.

I don't like some phases of life that I have seen in this city. I suspect, too, it is just exactly the same all over the whole world. People everywhere are trying to have a "good time" and ending in having a most miserably bad time. All that Dr. Beebe had said during his sermon seemed to roll off the consciences of Abby and Joe just as water does off our ducks' backs.

When we arrived at the Carter apartment, Abby and Joe were simply too sweet for words. So were the Carters. I wondered if ever I could pretend at sincere friendships as they were all doing, for I doubted the sincerity of the Carters. Of course, I was urged to play, but besides not knowing one card from the other, I didn't feel in the mood or physically able to play. Consequently, they urgently advised me to lie down on the divan while they played. I watched them for a while and tried to catch on to what they were supposed to be doing, but it was all so puzzling to me that I gave up and simply watched to see who seemed to be winning. At first they played for dimes. Then when they got more interested, they raised it to quarters. Joe seemed to be winning right along. He was quite hilarious. Abby was a problem. I didn't know whether she was pleased at Joe's success or not. Then when he raised the what-ever-it-is-called to a dollar, I knew that she was not pleased, for she had feared exactly this very thing. Joe was losing his head. The Carters saw it, too. I caught them glancing at each other, but Abby didn't see because she was too concerned about Joe and he didn't see because he was too excited about winning. He won the dollars twice. Then Mr. Carter carelessly laid down a five dollar bill! Joe covered it. His "luck" turned with that five dollar bill. I grew too weary of it all to watch any longer. And I was so thoroughly disgusted that I didn't want to watch. Joe's face was red, Abby's was white, Mr. Carter's mouth was as tight as bees' wax, and Mrs. Carter looked like a thunder cloud. I went to sleep.

It was one o'clock when Abby aroused me and said they were ready to go home. They bade farewell to the Carters so very affectionately that I supposed Joe and Abby had simply swept everything before them. But we had scarcely gotten in the car when the storm broke! We have had some pretty severe lightning and thunder storms with lots and lots of wind out in the hills, but I declare, I never, never saw anything to beat the storm of words that Abby and Joe had. They forgot all about me. I was thoroughly ashamed of both of them. I decided then and there that never, never would I quarrel with my husband as Abby was quarrelling with hers then. Of course, my husband and I should never have the same sort of reason for scrapping, for I certainly never intend to play bridge or any other gambling game, which is all that their bridge had been. It wasn't even a very polite game. It certainly did not end politely!

As all storms must cease some time, this one did, too, and they both apologized to me before we were really inside the house. I was too sleepy and tired to pay much attention to their apology. It didn't take me many seconds to get into my bed. Oh, how good it felt!

The next morning Abby awoke me. I felt stiff and sore and my head had a nice knot on it.

"Betsann, do you feel like getting up? Terry is on the wire. It is ten o'clock or I wouldn't have called you even for him," Abby told me.

Of course I got out of bed immediately. Since there was an upstairs connection, I did not have to dress before I could talk to Terry.

"Did I make you get up, honey? I am sorry, but I simply had to know how you are," Terry said, anxiously.

"I think I am all right," I replied. I hardly knew, but I seemed to feel about as usual. "How are you?"

"Well, I am rather stiff and sore. I was afraid you might be, too. I am glad to hear you say you are all right. Have you seen the morning papers?" he asked.

"No, not yet."

"They tell all about the accident. No one was killed, but several are very badly injured and are still in the hospital. I hope you won't mind my having to give your name to the press. It says we were in it, too, and that you received severe bruises about the head. You don't mind, do you?" he wanted to know.

"Why, no, certainly not. We were there and we did

get bumped, but my bruises aren't very severe, I think."

"Well, I am glad you are all right. Go on back to sleep. I'll be seeing you tonight. Bye, sweet," he whispered.

"Good-bye," I said, out loud.

Then I sought Abby.

"Have you read the morning papers?" I asked.

"Yes, I have. They tell about yesterday's accident. You are in it, too. When your mother and father read about this, they will be standing on their ears," Abby told me laughingly.

I didn't think it was a laughing matter, myself. She gave me the paper. There it was! Even the picture of the three cars. I didn't know any one had taken a picture. And there I was, too. With severe bruises about the head, even as Terry had said.

There was but one thing for me to do. Go home! And go home at once! The mail did not reach our part of the hills until after dinner. I could be there in a little while after it got there and Mom and Dad wouldn't have much time to worry. And what a marvelous excuse for going! There was not a single thing I wanted to do quite so much as I wanted to go home! "Abby, I'm going home just as soon as I can get started," I said, laying down the paper and proceeding to dress.

"What's your hurry? I thought you were going to stay until tomorrow morning. What are you going to do about Terry and the dance tonight?" she asked.

Terry and the dance! I was going home!

"Oh, I'll call him and explain as soon as I am ready to go. I think he will understand. I don't want Dad hiring a car and coming here to see about his darling daughter," I said, feeling better than I had felt since I had left home on Saturday.

I hurried. I didn't even eat much breakfast. Then when I was all ready, I telephoned Terry.

"I am starting home right now, Terry. I dare not stay, for Dad will be coming to Charlotte to see if I am still alive. I am sorry about not seeing you again, but you understand. Don't you?" I asked, trying not to sound too thrilled.

"Why, yes, I see how you feel about it. Do your folks get the Charlotte paper?" he asked.

"Yes, and that is the first thing Dad always reads. It comes shortly after dinner and he keeps on resting until he has seen his paper," I replied.

"In that case, I can see that you had better go. That is, if you are able. How about it?" he wanted to know.

"Oh, I'm fine! I still have a knot on my head, but I am perfectly all right," I assured him.

"Little lady, listen to me. I'm coming to see you. I'm coming this very next Sunday. I want to meet your mother and father and let them see the fellow they will have to call son some day. Does Abby know how to drive out there?" he asked, softly.

"Yes, they have been out," I told him, not knowing just how I did feel about it.

"Okay! I'll bring them along. They can entertain

your folks while you show me the country. Don't forget, honey," he murmured.

"I'll be looking for you. Good-bye, Terry," I hastened
to say.

"Bye, sweet. Be careful, and let me know if you
get home all right. I'll be watching for a letter right
away."

"Well," I said, as I hung up the receiver.

And I was gone! I was on my way home!

I drove very carefully, you may be sure, through the
city. I didn't even draw a good, long breath until I was
out on the highway where there seemed to be plenty
of room. Then I sighed, relaxed, and actually faced the
fact that I was going home, no longer the girl who had
left so few days before. I had seen life! I certainly had.
I had seen it from many different sides. And I knew
as well as I knew that I was driving Dad's old roadster
that I never, never could write successful stories about
most of the sorts that I had seen. If I should write such
stories, it would sound as if I approved of everything
about which I wrote. That would not be honest, for I
did not approve of it. Jimmy had been right.

Jimmy!

Why, Jimmy! Suddenly, like a flash, I realized that
Jimmy was in all probability married by this time. I
very nearly let the car stop. I might have run off the
pavement if a car behind me hadn't honked and
brought me to my senses again. Of course, he was married. He had said he would be in Asheville by the time
I got home. He had said he would be moving into the

old Miller place soon. He had said he wanted me to help him remodel it! I guess Libby Lou might not know just how to fix up an old log house! Libby Lou and Jimmy!

I drove more slowly. I needed lots of time to think things through. Did I want to live in Charlotte even though I did win that five hundred dollars? Would it not be a better investment to repair our house at home, paint it, and build a room all of my own where I could write without any interruptions? Jimmy had said that I could study life in the hills. Jimmy had said so many things. He had been right about entirely too many of them, too. I hated to admit it even to myself, but it was true. He had known I never would fit into the life at Charlotte.

But what about Terry? Terry! He was dear. He was almost as fine as Jimmy. Of course, Jimmy was different because he had been brought up in an entirely different atmosphere. If Terry had been a mountaineer, he probably would have been superior to Jimmy. Terry wasn't the sort of Christian that Jimmy was, but then perhaps he was the sort that fitted his life and profession better. But was he? Wouldn't Jimmy's brand of Christianity, and Libby Lou's Lord Jesus, be practical in Terry's life? Mrs. Simpson had been teaching a class of business girls on Sunday, but would she not have taught the same sort of lesson had it been a class of young business men? Perhaps Terry could be made to see how he, too, could live a deeply consecrated life and become a lawyer who would be known everywhere for his honesty, truthfulness, and devotion to the Lord. When he came out Sunday and I showed him the country, perhaps by that time, I could also show him the Master.

When was I going to become a Christian? Twice had the Lord definitely spared my life. Why? Oh, I was glad, I couldn't begin to tell how glad and thankful I am that He did spare my life, for I was not ready to die. Neither was I ready as I drove home from Charlotte on that Monday. I tried to search my heart to see if there was anything I could not give up for the Lord's sake. It was different from what it had been. Before, I did not want to give up my career as a writer of high-life stories. I still wanted a career. I still wanted to write. I wanted to write about folks who make the whole world better because they are living. I never would be ashamed then to have to claim one of my stories as my own "brain child." To do that sort of writing, I should need the help of the Lord Himself! I realized this quite suddenly, just as I was realizing many things suddenly. Just as soon after I was home and settled as I possibly could, I would surrender to the Lord! Perhaps that very night, if Cherry did not want to sleep with me as she often did when I was away for a few days and then came back.

Cherry! She was a Christian. I'd ask her just exactly what she did to accept the Lord as her Saviour. Every one says it is so simple, but it is not to me. Just what does it mean to accept the Lord? I am not so stupid that I don't know what it means to accept something tangible, but this other acceptance is different. "A little child shall lead them." I would let Cherry lead me!

Then, after Terry had really become an out-and-out Christian and we knew each other better, perhaps then, maybe in several years, after I had learned a little how to write and how to live a really consecrated life, why, then, we might be married. Of course, we'd have to live in Charlotte, but that could be delightful, too. There would be Dorothea, and I was sure she would soon be as consecrated a Christian as even Mrs. Simpson would want. Then I could know Mrs. Simpson. There would be many of her kind that we should know and love. A different sort of life we would live then, for we would be different people and enjoy different things. Yes, that would be just right!

When I had reached all these conclusions, I gave the old engine a little more gas and made better time. I wasn't feeling any too well, but I did not realize it as I thought and thought and tried to decide so many things. When I did let go of myself and give my attention only to the car, I knew that I was just about as nearly sick as I like to be while I am away from home and driving all alone. I thought of praying. I wished I could! I knew if I could pray and ask the Lord Jesus to help me get home, He would. But what right had I to ask him? I was no child of His—yet. I had no more real right to ask Him for help than a perfect stranger would have to ask my Dad for help. I set my teeth and drove faster. I was within ten miles of home and if I did become too ill to drive on, I easily could stop and ask someone I knew to take me home. If I just didn't faint or something while I was driving! All sorts of silly ideas popped into my poor aching head.

I managed to keep going and stay in the road. No one passed me. Finally I could see Jimmy's house about half a mile away. I wished I could run in there and get him to take me home. But he was in Asheville! Or was it Charlotte? Just where was he? I thought I saw a big, new, shining car turn into the highway from his side road. I slowed down, for I did not want to bump into it. It looked dreadfully huge, as if it took up all the road. I wondered whose it was and where they were going. It came on towards me with full speed. I pulled out to the side of the road and stopped. I just knew it was going to smash me if I kept on going! It came on, apparently not going to slow down at all. I could see that there were four people in it, two men and two women. It looked like Jimmy in front at the wheel. It looked like my Mom, it looked like my Dad in the back! It looked—

When I looked again, I was in my own room at home. There sitting beside my bed was my own Mom! I must have looked at her rather strangely, for she kissed me and said, "You are all right now, little girl!"

Of course I was! What was I doing in my bed and what was she sitting there for? I looked around the room and then tried to smile at Mom.

" What happened?" I asked.

"When we got the paper today and saw that you had been in a car wreck, your dad went over and got

Jimmy to take us to Charlotte to see about you," Mom said, gently.

"Jimmy?" I gasped.

"Yes, darling. Jimmy has a new car and he and Marjorie were just ready to start to Asheville to the wedding when your dad got there. They dropped every plan, though, and we were just starting to see about you when we met you in the road. You had stopped the car in a ditch and then fainted. Jimmy picked you up, put you in your dad's lap, and brought us home. Are you better now, dearie?"

"Yes, I'm all right. Where are Jimmy and the others now?" I wanted to know.

"He and Marjorie were awfully sorry, but they had to go on to Asheville. It's to be a big church wedding and they had to rehearse for it this evening. Your dad had gone back—"

I didn't hear any more right then, for I proceeded to faint again. I certainly was being silly! The next time I opened my eyes, Mom and Dad and Cherry were all standing beside the bed. They looked scared.

"Hello, Dad. Hello, Cherry," I tried to say.

Cherry burst out crying and ran from the room. Dad took my hand and held it gently.

"Where does it hurt, Elizabeth?" he asked, rather brokenly. He never calls me Elizabeth unless he wants to be very, very kind to me. It's my special pet name from him.

"Why, no place, Dad. Only my head. It aches. I

guess I was just tired," I said, feeling a little better. "And I'm hungry!"

"Bless your heart," my Mom exclaimed, wiping tears from her precious eyes. "Haven't you had any dinner?"

"No, I didn't eat breakfast till after ten and not much then. What time is it now?" I asked.

"It's nearly five! You lie still and I'll bring you something in a minute. Dad, you stay with her so if she wants anything she can tell you," Mom said, as she left the room.

She had no more than reached the kitchen when the door opened and in stepped Dr. Bostick.

"What's going on here?" he asked, in his usual good humor, approaching my bed and shaking hands with Dad. "What have you been up to?"

I wanted to giggle and cry, too. "Oh, I've been on a trip to the big city of Charlotte," I managed to say.

"It looks as if the big city had not been very kind to you," he said, touching my bumped head. "Were you struck any other place?"

"Only my head, as far as I know. I am not broken any place," I told him.

"You feel pretty silly and weepy and shaken up?" he asked. That's exactly how I felt. He said that he thought it was my nerves more than my head and that I should stay in bed for several days and sleep a lot and eat and drink lots of milk. Then I'd be as good as new.

"I won't die, will I, Doctor?" I asked, as he finished telling us all that.

Mom came into the room as I asked the question. Glancing at her, I saw her almost drop the tray she held and she turned pale.

"Oh, no, you aren't likely to die from this bump, but I'd advise you not to try another one soon," he replied laughingly.

Mom recovered. And you don't know how relieved I was. I didn't want to die. I wasn't ready yet to die. I wasn't even ready to live, but I wanted to live till I was ready.

I ate a big dinner-supper and was sleepy right away. Doctor Bostick said that sleep was the very best tonic I could have. He told me to nestle down, relax, and let go of everything and sleep.

"I won't die while I'm asleep, will I?" I just couldn't help asking.

"No, you are a lot better already. Sleep will make you well more quickly than anything else. Get dying out of your head. You aren't really sick," he reassured me, feeling my pulse.

I was sick all right, but not physically sick. But I went to sleep, for I intended to settle this great question of my salvation as soon as I woke up again. I just would not keep putting it off. Then I was gone.

It was morning and the sun was shining when I awoke! I was so surprised. Mom slipped into the room before I could decide to get up.

"Stay right in that bed, daughter," she said, sitting down beside me. "How do you feel?"

"Grand, Mom! Please let me get up," I coaxed.

"Not yet. Stay still until afternoon and then if you feel all right, you may try it."

"Mom, how did Dr. Bostick happen to come?" I remembered to ask.

"Jimmy and Marjorie stopped on their way to Asheville and told him," she said.

"When is the wedding?" I murmured.

"This morning at ten."

"What time is it now?"

"Nine-twenty-six," she said, looking at my little clock.

"It's almost time!" I sighed.

"Just about. Libby Lou will be a lovely bride. I'd like to have seen her," Mom said, gazing out the window.

"Yes, she will. Mom, have I any mail?" I asked, remembering "Fragrant as Lilacs."

"None that amounts to anything," she told me.

"My story, there isn't anything about it?"

"No, not a word!"

"I wish I'd hear from it," I said, I'm afraid rather peevishly. I had suddenly begun to feel cross.

"You will surely hear from it soon. I am going to send Cherry in with your breakfast now, and you be a good girl and stay in bed, maybe all day."

"Well," was all I said.

If Cherry brought my breakfast, maybe I could ask her some questions. I just wouldn't let myself think about the wedding, even if it was right at ten o'clock.

And, would you believe it? I began to cry like a regular silly baby!

CHAPTER XII

WHEN Cherry came in, I was still crying. I didn't know exactly why, but I was. Still my nerves, I guess, as Dr. Bostick had said.

"Why, Sis, what's the matter?" stammered Cherry, as she set the tray on my little table. "Mom said you were a whole lot better and here you are crying."

"I am better, Cherry. I hardly know why I am crying. Don't tell Mom. I felt fine when I first woke up. Maybe I haven't slept enough yet. I'll try it again when I eat my breakfast. You are a dear little sister to bring it to me," I said, as I sat up and prepared to eat.

"Well, Mom said to bring it. She said did you want anything else?" Poor Cherry looked worried.

"No, dear, I have more here than I can eat. You help me, won't you?"

She shook her head. "Mom said for you to eat every bite, 'cause Dr. Bostick said for you to eat a whole lot. Sis, you are going to get well, 'cause I have been asking Jesus to make you well. And I just know He will."

There! That was what was the matter with me. I hadn't yet found out how to let Jesus come into my heart.

"I am glad I am going to be well, Cherry. It was sweet of you to ask Jesus to help me to get all right," I said, intending to keep on till I had asked her the all-important question.

"Why, Sis, didn't you ask Him, too? I just know Mom and Dad have. Why, yesterday when Dad read that in the paper about you, it just seemed like everything in the whole world was wrong. Even Dad cried a little teensy bit. He didn't take time to cry much, though, for he lit out after Jimmy as fast as he could go before he had time to cry much. Mom and I kept on crying after he had gone, but we didn't have much time, 'cause I had to put on a clean dress so's to stay with Mrs. Casper and Mom had to get ready to go to Charlotte. You beat 'em though, and they didn't get to go." She chuckled a little as she remembered that. "Then the world didn't seem so all wrong and I asked Jesus some more to make you well. Sis, you have asked Him, too, haven't you?"

"Not yet, Cherry," I admitted slowly, trying to think just how to ask her my question.

"Why, I'd think you'd have asked Him that the very first thing! Why haven't you asked Him, Sis?"

"Cherry, put this tray there on the table and then come and sit down by me and tell me something," I began. She did as I asked her and then sat on the edge of my bed.

"What do you want me to tell you?" she asked, her lovely brown eyes big and wondering.

"Cherry, I want you to tell me just exactly how you

let Jesus come into your heart. How did you know when He came? Are you sure He did come?" I asked, watching her expressive little face. At the first question she smiled. Then she became a little serious. Finally she looked just a little puzzled. I suspect I should not have asked so many at one time. It wasn't at all what I had expected to ask.

"Why, I guess I let Jesus come into my heart just like I let any one else come in that I love a whole lot. I guess when you love any one just heaps and heaps and heaps he's bound to be in your heart. And that's how I love Jesus! I love Mom and Dad and you and Libby Lou and Jimmy and lots of folks and you are all in my heart. Well, I love Jesus better'n all the rest of you put together, so He's in my heart, too. I knew He was in there when I began loving Him so much, just like I knew Libby Lou was in there when I began to love her such a heap. And of course I'm sure He came into my heart. I guess I know when I love some one and I know I love Him and I know that He came into my heart and I know He's still there and I know He will always and always and always be there. Why, Sis, what did you ask me all those questions for? Isn't He in your heart too?"

"Not yet, Cherry, but I want Him to come in," I admitted.

"Why, Elizabeth Ann Ellison, don't you love Jesus?" asked my little sister, surprised as if I had acknowledged that I didn't love Mom or Dad.

"Yes, I do love Him. But didn't you do anything

about it? Didn't you tell Him you loved Him? Didn't you ask Him to forgive your sins, though what sins a little girl like you could have is more than I can see. Is loving Jesus all there is to being a Christian?" I kept on.

Cherry propped her feet against a chair, hugged her knees up close, and looked very thoughtful as she answered me, "Yes, I told Jesus I loved Him and I asked Him please to forgive all my sins. Why, Sis, I had a lot of sins to be forgiven. Don't you know that I had sassed Mom and even Dad? I'd stuck out my tongue at you more than once when you made me mad and I pulled Susan's hair once at school and I told Miss Mary a story about eating an apple in school and I had a lot of sins to be forgiven for. Well, I was sorry when I saw that I was lost and would go to hell if I didn't repent and ask Jesus to save me and let Him come into my heart forever and ever. So I did. I prayed and He says He will forgive if we ask Him to so I just know He forgave me and washed me white as snow like the song says. Then I felt all good inside of me when I knew He had forgiven me and had come into my heart and saved me.

"I've tried to be better since then. I read my Testament every single day and I pray every single night before I go to bed. I don't even want to pull Susan's hair any more and I try to mind Mom better. Sometimes I do get mad and I feel like saying things that Jesus might not want me to say. Then I pray a little bit and I feel better. I guess that's when the old bad man comes knocking at my heart's door and tells me to be bad again. But when I pray, I guess Jesus goes to the door and when the old bad man sees Jesus, he just scoots and leaves me alone. Sis, did I answer your questions?"

"Yes, I think you have. You love Jesus. You asked Him to forgive your sins. You asked Him to come into your heart and save you. Then you trusted that He had done all that you had asked Him to do. Is that it?" I asked again, for I wanted to be sure for my own benefit.

"Yes, you see the Bible says to trust Jesus and believe in Him and I did and I still do. Can't you do all that, too?" she asked, looking me squarely in the eyes. "Our T verse last Sunday was 'Trust in the Lord.' And when we had B it was 'Be not afraid, only believe.' And I guess that's all there is to being a Christian and being saved. Don't you? So can't you do that?"

"Yes, I can!" I exclaimed. "And I will! Cherry, let's you and me kneel down here by my bed and ask the Lord Jesus to forgive my sins and come into my heart. Will you, honey? I've been wanting to be a Christian for a long time, but I have been too stubborn to admit it."

Well, I was crying again. Seems to me that I was doing a lot of crying those days. I seldom cry, but I certainly did a lot then. Dear little Cherry scampered off my bed and knelt before I could get out. Then I knelt beside her and put my arm around her and drew her close. She was crying, too, a little bit.

"Dear Jesus, please help my Sis to let You come into

her heart. She's not a bad girl at all, but please forgive her sins and save her like You did me. And thank You, Jesus. For Jesus' sake, Amen!" prayed Cherry as earnestly as ever I had heard any one pray.

For a little bit I couldn't pray. Finally I controlled myself and did manage to pray a little prayer, "Dear Lord Jesus, I am not worthy to ask Thee to forgive me, for I've been so stubborn and hard-headed, but do please forgive me. I want to be a Christian. I want Thee to come into my heart. O God, I do surrender everything to Thee. I want my whole life to count for Thee. Please accept me and save me." I had to wait a minute. And while I waited, there was the sweetest peace that filled my whole being! I never had felt quite like that. I knew that Jesus had heard my prayer and that He had saved me. I was happy. "Oh, thank Thee, Jesus!" I cried. Then I hugged Cherry and she hugged me.

"See, Sis, when Jesus saves you, you do know it. Don't you?" she asked, her face aglow.

"I do, Cherry. I don't know about other people, but I know that He has saved me and I am glad. And little sister, you helped me, oh so much!" I told her, kissing her pink cheeks.

Well, we talked a little bit more and I said maybe I'd better go to sleep again and then I'd get up after a while if Mom said I could. She took the tray and left me. I had a song in my heart and I sang it till I went to sleep. This was the song:

*"What a wonderful change in my life has been
  wrought,
Since Jesus came into my heart!
I have light in my soul for which long I had
  sought,
Since Jesus came into my heart,*

*"Since Jesus came into my heart,
Since Jesus came into my heart,
Floods of joy o'er my soul like the sea billows
  roll,
Since Jesus came into my h-e-a-r——"*

I was asleep and I slept till after noon. I felt so much
better! Mom came slipping into my room again.

"I'm hungry!" I announced. "Please let me get up!"

Mom kissed me. Cherry must have told her about
our little time together, for Mom's face had a sweet,
understanding expression. We never have been much
of a family to talk to each other. I'm going to begin
right away to talk to my children so that when they
grow up, they still will think of me as their chum.

"Will you keep very quiet and lie down again if you
begin to feel at all sick?" Mom asked.

Of course I promised. And I stayed up till early bed-
time. Billy brought me a note from Terry and one from
Dorothea. I had forgotten all about writing to Terry!
But then I couldn't have written if I had remembered.

And Jimmy! And Mrs. Jimmy Casper! Had they gone
on a honeymoon? When would they be back? It would

seem so queer, having Jimmy married! But, then, that was something for me to pray about. We had grown up together and he was like a brother to me, that was all; yet I certainly did feel, well, maybe a little jealous of Libby Lou. That was the first time I had acknowledged it even to myself. Now jealousy must have no place in my life!

I wrote Terry a letter before I went to bed. I promised Dad I'd pick cotton again in the morning. He said he'd see.

When I awoke on Wednesday morning, the sun was up. What was making me so sleepy-headed? The first thing I saw was a most gorgeous bunch of dahlias on my table. I knew at once they did not grow anywhere around us. I dressed quickly and went to the kitchen. Mom was feeding the chickens, but Cherry was there.

"Where did those wonderful dahlias come from?" I asked the very first thing.

"Marjorie brought them to you last night after you had gone to sleep. She said she was late geting home, but that she just had to come and see how you were. Libby Lou sent you those flowers. She had a whole lot of them at the wedding, Marjorie said. Aren't they just grand?"

I wanted to ask if Jimmy had come, too, but I didn't. I'd find out more soon enough! Mom wouldn't let me pick cotton. She said I still looked a little pale.

When it was about time for Billy, I strolled to the mail box, taking Terry's letter to mail. And that's how

it happened that I received the long, slender envelope
my very own self.

"You feelin' better?" Billy asked, as he handed me
the mail.

I could hardly answer him, for I was so excited. In
my hand I held the verdict on "Fragrant as Lilacs."

"Yes, I'm fine again," I did manage to say, as I turned
around.

"Better not be gaddin' 'round with them Charlotte
fellers. Better stick to the fellers up here," Billy advised,
as he shifted and drove off.

With trembling fingers I tore open the long, slender
envelope.

I nearly died right then and there! All alone, there
by the mail box! I sank to the bank and stared at the
letter. Then I pulled myself up and staggered into the
woods, where I had a favorite retreat. I read that letter
again after I had sat upon my rock and leaned against
a strong old oak.

"Fragrant as Lilacs" had been retained for recon-
sideration after the judges had decided not to give it
the prize. Finally it was found not available for pub-
lication and was being returned by express collect. If
I would keep up my writing and have it criticized by
an expert critic, there was no doubt in the writer's
mind but that some day I would become a full-fledged
authoress. I had their very best wishes!

I can't begin to tell you how I felt! All my hopes
were crushed. I felt utterly undone, weak, sick, alone,
perfectly miserable. I lay flat on my rock, my face

buried in my arms, the letter at my side. I wept and I wept bitterly this time. I couldn't pray. I couldn't do anything but cry hard.

I didn't hear any footsteps. I didn't know anyone was near me, until I heard a low whistle and a rustling of paper. Someone had found me and someone had found my letter! Oh, I simply could not rise up and face whoever it was! Why, why didn't he or she go off and leave me alone.

Someone sat down beside me and placed a hand on my shoulders. It felt like such a sympathetic hand that I wept anew. Not a word was spoken. The hand just patted and patted my shoulders until I grew a little calmer.

"Betsann, old timer, you've cried enough now. You'll make yourself worse again. Come on, brace up! You are no silly little baby!" a voice said, gently but firmly.

It sounded like Jimmy!

I listened, but I couldn't bear to look up. Suppose it was Jimmy! He belonged to Libby Lou and he would only pity me. But suppose it was not Jimmy! I couldn't bear to have anyone else I knew find me like this.

"This is the best thing I've seen in ages, Bets. What a lot of encouragement this letter holds! Suppose you had won that measly little old five hundred dollars. You would never have known how to keep on and improve till you became the writer that you really want to become. Buck up, old girl, you'll show the world yet what you can do!" the voice continued, all the world like Jimmy.

I peeped.

It was Jimmy!

He turned me over and made me sit up.

"Let me wipe away those unbecoming tears," he said, wiping my eyes with his own handkerchief. He had on his old overalls and grey work shirt. He didn't look a bit like a new groom. "There, that's better! Aside from the disappointment which this old letter naturally must have caused you, how are you feeling?"

"I'm lots better," I managed to say, gathering myself out of his reach and adjusting my hair.

"I am glad to hear it. We hurried home just as fast as we could after that old wedding, because I was worried about you. Marjorie came to see you last night, but I stayed at home and did the chores that were still to do, because I thought you'd likely be asleep. What did Doc say about your injuries?" he asked, leaning against the old oak, just as he had done dozens of times before.

"He said it was my nerves more than my bumps. I've done a lot of sleeping and eating as he said for me to do," I said, trying to screw up courage enough to ask about his wife.

"I'm glad you didn't have any internal injuries. This news today isn't the best in the world for your nerves, either, unless you look at it in the right way. Bets, I never was so thrilled over anything in all my born days, believe it or not. I guess you won't be going to Charlotte to live now very soon. Will you?" he asked, and he had the nerve to grin as if he were as glad as glad could be.

"No, I guess not, but anyway, I had already decided that I wouldn't go to Charlotte very soon. You see— well, Jimmy, I might as well tell you that I have changed my mind entirely about the sort of life that I want to write about. After I had seen life as I thought I wanted to see it, I decided that it wasn't my kind at all and that I never could write about it because I never could live it. And anyway, Jimmy, I'm not the same sort of girl I was when I went to Charlotte this last time. You see, I am a Christian now. I have surrendered my whole life to the Lord Jesus and I am going to stay right here and write stories about people who make the world better because they have lived. And maybe I can help you and Libby Lou a little in the church and Sunday School," I finally told him.

"Hold on, Bets! You are telling me so much that I can't grasp it all. Do you mean it when you say you are a Christian?" asked Jimmy, looking as if he could simply eat me alive.

I nodded my head. "Yes, I mean it. I gave my heart to the Lord Jesus just yesterday. I had wanted to do it for a long time, but I was too wrapped up in what I thought was my career and I just knew that kind of a career would not be the right kind for a real Christian and I didn't want to be any half-way Christian. So I held out and stayed miserable all the time, trying to have my own way and persuade myself that it was the best way for me. But now I see things differently. I want only His way," I said, and I held my head high as I said it, for I certainly did mean it.

"Bets, I'm perfectly speechless, I am so glad and happy. I'd shout till the echo would ring plumb to home if I wasn't scared someone would think I had found you dead or something. I just knew you weren't happy. Why, Bets, you couldn't ever have lived the sort of life you thought you wanted to live. You are too sweet and good and, oh, gee, Bets, I just can't say all I want to say!" Jimmy Casper for once in his life couldn't express himself.

I thought it was time to bring him to himself again and find something he could express himself on, so I asked, "Where is Libby Lou? Was she a lovely bride? Did you get scared and drop the ring, or didn't you have a ring service?"

You should have seen Jimmy's face! It was too funny for words. The more questions I asked, the funnier it got.

"Betsann, you silly goose, do you think it was *my* wedding?" he finally asked me.

"Why, yes, certainly I think it was your wedding, yours and Libby Lou's!" I replied, sweetly.

Well, Jimmy laughed till he cried. "Of all the things I ever heard in all my born days!" he at last recovered enough to say. "Didn't you get an invitation to the wedding?"

"No, I did not," I told him.

"How come? One was sent you. Libby Lou said she sent it and she thought you might come to the wedding with Marjorie and me. She was right disappointed because you didn't come. Listen to me, Bets Ann Ellison, I *did not* get married yesterday and not today either, though I am about to be soon, I think!" he added, looking for all the world like a mischievous boy.

"Really? Who is the unfortunate girl?" I asked, trying to match his mood.

"That is for you to say! Bets, are you going to marry that Charlotte guy?" Jimmy asked, all the fun, all the joking gone from his face, as he moved a little nearer to me.

"What Charlotte guy?" I asked, teasing him a little, for I had been teased a plenty.

"Oh, you know! That lawyer feller. The one you said was *the* man. You aren't going to marry him now. Are you, Bets?" he asked, and I thought he was about to cry.

"No, not now!" I said, smiling at him.

"Not now and not ever?" he persisted.

"He is coming Sunday to become acquainted with Mom and Dad," I suddenly remembered.

"You write him to stay in Charlotte where he belongs! You know as well as I do that you belong to me and have ever since you were born. Didn't I kiss you when you were a teensy baby when no one was looking? I was the first boy to kiss you and I'm going to be the last. Let's get married tomorrow, Bets!" pled Jimmy, pulling me closer to him.

Tomorrow! How could I?

"Not tomorrow, Jimmy," I said, pretending to be

joking, but never had my heart beat faster and never had I felt so perfectly contented.

Then I remembered!

I couldn't marry Jimmy at all! It might be months and months before I could marry him! I thought sure I was going to cry again.

"What's the matter, Bets? You look as if something hurt you," Jimmy said, taking both my hands in his.

"Oh, Jimmy, I can't marry you or anyone else. I forgot—" I murmured miserably.

"What did you forget?"

"That old typewriter! I still owe a lot of money on it and I can't get married till it's paid for!" I gulped, swallowing hard to keep back my too-ready tears.

Well, Jimmy up and kissed me good and plenty!

"Betsann, I'll give you that typewriter for your wedding present if you will marry me tomorrow," Jimmy said at last.

"Really?" I asked.

"Really, truly!"

"Oh, but I can't marry you tomorrow. What's your hurry?"

"I don't want to give you time to get up a church wedding! One's enough in my lifetime. Let's just go down to the preacher's house and not have so much fuss. I just thought I'd die dead before Libby Lou's wedding was over. I was so worried about you and then everything had to be just so."

"Jimmy, what were you since you weren't the groom?" I asked, nestling against his comfortable shoulder. I felt happy and contented and so rested, as if another tremendous burden had been lifted. It was simply the completion of my feeling yesterday when I surrendered my life to the Lord Jesus. Oh, suppose I hadn't let Him come into my heart! Jimmy never would have been willing to marry me, for I remembered that he said the Bible teaches that a Christian should never marry someone who isn't a Christian. How good my Lord was! How thankful I was that I did not put off His precious gift of eternal life any longer! I forgot everything in my new perfected happiness.

"Well, I was an usher. Marjorie was one of the bridesmaids. Libby Lou married a young preacher and because he had to go to his new pastorate right away, the wedding was hurried up a little. But it is a whole lot of foolishness, Bets. We don't want all that fuss. Do we? Please let's get married tomorrow. Then we'll go right to the old Miller place and do all the things we have been planning," he coaxed.

"Tomorrow is Thursday. Let's wait till Saturday, Jimmy. That would give me a little time to get ready and a girl always likes to be a little ready," I put him off.

"Saturday it is, then, and it has to be early, too! We'll go to the preacher's house and then we'll go to Charlotte on our honeymoon and I'll buy you a typewriter for your wedding present! Is it a bargain?" he asked, making me look at him.

"Yes," I said, simply.

After a while, Jimmy said, "Bets, Beloved, if ever we

become troubled about anything at all, let's pray it through together. We both know that our God hears and answers prayer. He has proved it to us today. I am not perfect. You are as nearly perfect as anyone ever is, but I wouldn't be surprised if there is a little bit of imperfection about you! I think we are going to get along better than any two people who have ever loved each other. I am sure you think so, too. But there may be a time when we can't see everything eye to eye. If there is, let's not quarrel and be angry with each other. Let's pray about it and discuss it prayerfully and be willing to have God's way and not ours. Shall we?"

"Yes, Jimmy! I want us to put the Lord Jesus first in everything about our new lives," I said in no uncertain tones.

"Amen! Listen, here is my own personal verse, 'I have been crucified with Christ, and it is no longer I that live, but Christ that lives in me; and the life which I now live in the body I live through faith in the Son of God who loved me and gave Himself up to death on my behalf.' That is from my New Testament in Modern Speech by Weymouth. It is the twentieth verse of the second chapter of Galatians. I want my Lord Jesus Christ to live out His life in me. And in you," he added, as he drew me from the ground and kissed me as if it were in benediction.

So here is the announcement of our wedding! We did get married on Saturday. We did go to Charlotte and Rust came forward to meet me as usual. I was so proud to introduce my husband to him, for Jimmy looked simply handsome in his Libby Lou wedding suit! Rust was grand. He gave us our announcements for our wedding gift.

On Sunday Abby and Joe, Rust and Terry and Dot and the little girl they called Kitty all came out and brought a wedding feast that was fit for a queen and king. We had a perfectly grand time. I told them that I not only was married, but was married to a man who was an out-and-out Christian and that I, too, had accepted the Lord Jesus as my own Saviour and had surrendered my life to Him. Dorothea was so happy that she almost cried and said that she was not going to live a worldly life any longer. The others were rather serious looking, but no one else committed himself in any way.

And now we are living in the old Miller place. We are fixing it up so that there will be room enough for a whole bunch of the young folks to come for play-parties and good times. We want it to be their home as well as our own. And I am so happy!

We aren't going to have a really, truly honeymoon now. Maybe next summer Jimmy's new car will still be good enough and we can drive clear out to California! It's my car, too! So even if I didn't win that old five hundred dollars I won even greater prizes, I won Jimmy, and my Lord Jesus gave me salvation. What could be better?